For My Ariella, Ayelet, Yael, Shaya, Shlomo, and Max

Dedicated to Michael Evans

First Printing, 2015

ISBN: 978-0692529461

William Evans Publishing

Table of Contents

ABRAHAM'S SHIELD

Introduction

Over 3 million soldiers fought in some capacity during The American Civil War, according to most estimates. There was a small, but significant contribution made by the Jewish population, for both the North and South, towards the prosecution of the war from its inception, until its close. Jewish warriors had obtained ranks as high as Major General on the Union side and Secretary of War on the Confederate. In all, 10,000 out of a total population of 150,000 Jews took up arms. It is interesting to note that their part in the war and its outcome was disproportionately large, as evidenced by the high number of Jews receiving the Medal of Honor.

The chance encounter of two Jews fighting on opposite sides of the conflict may have made for some very interesting outcomes and no doubt would have influenced events far into the future. The intermingling of ancient traditions and modern thought would have occurred with consequences not fully understood at the time. In fact, not only would the history of the war have changed, but perhaps the individuals involved and their families would change as well for generations to come.

A little background on this historic battle is in order:

The day was May 1st, 1863 and the battle of Chancellorsville was in full swing. General Hooker had brought his troops across the Rappahannock River in an attempt at nothing less than the complete discomfiture and destruction of General Lee's fine Army of Northern Virginia.

The past years of war had brought mostly defeat to the blue side. Starting with the first Battle of Bull Run and culminating with the miserable mud march under Burnside two months prior, the fate of the North had seemed quite bleak, and that of the Confederacy was encouraging, to say the least. Southern independence seemed one victory away.

This time might be different however. Under a new commander, General "Fighting Joe" Hooker, the Army of the Potomac, at over 130,000 strong, was perched on the cusp of victory. They had successfully surrounded an enemy inferior in number and equipment. Lee had been unable to counter the thrust across the river at Fredericksburg and had instead divided his army in the presence of a superior foe, and attacked a force that was at least twice his size, and was bearing down on his flank. True, the Union right wing had paused upon being assaulted, but not for long. It was poised to steamroll the Confederate forces and with it any hopes of secession and Confederate independence.

Note: The bulk of our story takes place during the famous battle of Chancellorsville, when such a meeting may have taken place. It begins though, high above the Atlantic Ocean in seat 23b, aboard an El-Al flight headed towards Israel.

Chapter One

Aaron Heller unbuckled his seatbelt as the sign in the cabin flickered off. He groaned and stretched his long legs under the seat, being careful not to kick the person in front of him. It was going to be a long flight; nine and a half hours to Israel in all, and he was already growing antsy. This propensity for fidgeting was a Heller family trait dating back at least as far as Great, Great, Great Grandfather Hershel Heller of Civil War fame. Nearly 150 years ago he had been given the Medal of Honor for his actions, which stemmed from his adventurous nature.

Aaron reached into the overhead compartment after brushing against the person seated next to him. He apologized, but merely received a grunt in return.

Rummaging through his carry-on, he found the object he had been searching for. It was an old tome, perhaps twice as thick as a pack of cards and about the area of a small Android tablet. It was worn and rough to the touch, and had clearly seen better days. Yet for something that was 150 years old, it was still in excellent condition.

This object was his reminder of home and comfortable times as he visited the Jewish homeland for the first time. His grandfather Joe had given it to him just before he ducked into the cab on the way to the airport.

"Keep this with you, Aaron." He intoned seriously. "It has served our family well for many, many years, and it now it goes with you to the Holy Land"

Aaron blew the thin patina of dust from the plastic jacket that covered most of it and leafed through it, stopping at the smudged inscription for just a second:

5-3-1863 Inst.
To my dear friend Hans,
May this siddur serve you through all the trials, tribulations, and the good times as well, which you will face in the future. May Hashem bless you and keep you in all you do.
Truly, Your friend Levy
[J1]

The meaning behind this inscription was heavy. It carried with it over three thousand years of persecution and strength of national character. As Aaron sat down again, he opened the prayer book to the wayfarer's prayer and began to recite it softly in Hebrew: "Yehi Ratzon…"

The person sitting next to him clucked his tongue while looking with disdain at his fellow traveler. "Ancient superstitions!" he mumbled under his breath, "Never helped anyone before, and it won't now, either."

"I'm sorry, what was that?" Aaron asked his surly traveling companion.

"Nothing. I didn't mean to interrupt you, but I can't understand why you people always have to be praying or reciting something or other. What is all this stuff to you?"

This was beginning to sound like a question Aaron had heard before at his Passover Seder and he was wondering whether he'd have to blunt this man's teeth like the wicked son at some point soon.

"This prayer actually asks God to make sure we have a safe trip, yourself included. Just a simple prayer is all. Does that upset you?"

"No, but I think you are... how do you say, wasting your time! There's no one up there," he continued on, while pointing up at the ceiling with an expansive gesture. "Or anywhere, that will stop something from happening--good or bad."

Aaron sized up his traveling companion with trepidation. His buzz cut, shiny shirt, tight jeans, and apathetic look all alluded to his character. His type is the Israeli who is too macho to be afraid; he's seen the world and all that. His appearance was that of someone of perhaps 30, but in all actuality, was probably ten years older. A certain glimmer in his eye betrayed a keen intelligence.

Aaron couldn't resist any longer. The time had come to tell "the story," but before that, he thought it best to introduce himself. "I didn't catch your name." Aaron said.

"My name's Avi." replied the man seated next to him.

"So Ah, Avi, would you like to hear the history behind this book?" he said, pointing to the volume in his hand. "You may learn something.

Chapter Two

As the old adage goes, "There's no such thing as an atheist in a foxhole," and that's been true since before they were called foxholes. Hans (Hershel) Heller was soon to discover this for himself, although he didn't know it yet.

Hans had been part of the grand wheel[1] [J5] around the left of Lee's Army of Northern Virginia. Most of the movement had been marching and camping. A few light skirmishes here and there, but no major battle to speak of when the crossing had been made.

Due to his special position, even marching was exciting. An intelligence officer and occasional spy behind enemy lines like Hans had constant stimulation. Being quick-witted and spry came in handy in that line of work. Make a wrong move and it was over. No mercy or conventional rules of war applied to spies. A Kangaroo court and a quick dangle from a rope was what one could expect if he was lucky.

Now, as Hans peered out over the Wilderness, that strange feeling came over him again. The feeling of excitement, mixed with anxious curiosity, began to well up inside him. Which new ways would he find to evade capture? How would he avoid being detained while still gaining valuable information that might mean the difference between victory and defeat? Only the future would tell. But one thing was certain; a grand adventure waited.

Hans turned to his fellow special services officer, Patrick Mcgivern and expressed these feelings in his usual off-hand manner. As they both sat atop their horses, Pat grunted and spit out a wad of tobacco he had been mushing around in his mouth. The oily, black juice kicked up a spurt of dust before settling as a dark smudge on the dirt path. He was never much for feelings. All action and grim determination; *that* was Pat.

They had been through several firefights and tight squeezes together, and helped each other in countless other ways. There was that one time when they helped steal a train all the way down in Georgia, and Pat helped Hans avoid a posthumous medal. Or when they both became trapped behind enemy lines during the Second Battle of Manassas, and Hans' unusual choice of clothing saved the day. Also, Pat didn't care that Hans was Jewish. Didn't mind it in the least. "A fellow was a fellow," he'd say, and didn't give a darn what anybody thought of his

---

[1] Military term used during the 19th Century referring to a movement of the entire army in an arch-like fashion around an obstacle or opposing force.

opinions.

That wasn't the case for some of the soldiers Hans had to associate with, however. His commanding officer had called him a "dirty Jew" to his face in front of the other men and most had laughed. A few of his fellow soldiers had even spit at the ground to show their disdain. Pat had been the only one to stick up for him, and even so much as stayed with him on Christmas day while the other men went to mass and had their turkey dinner. Hans guessed that must have been hard, but he didn't say anything to Pat that night, aside from "Happy Holidays."

A shot whizzed by their heads right between the two horses at eye level. Time to take cover. One shot from a sniper that didn't hit its mark, meant more to come until either the target fled or became the former occupier of an empty saddle and pair of boots. Dashing into the nearby thicket, the two friends regrouped under some trees. What would the future battle bring? It was anyone's guess at this point. Still, one had to wonder.

Chapter Three

Across the fields in a generally eastern direction, General Robert E. Lee glanced once more at his map before hoisting a pair of binoculars to his eyes. As usual, his dove-grey uniform was impeccably tailored and fastidiously clean. While most of his soldiers wore butternut rags, the general felt that first he had to command respect, even in his dress, and his cat-like love for cleanliness would not allow him to be dressed in anything but his best. His antagonist, the Army of the Potomac, had stopped where it was and declined to advance. Lee had sensed a bit of hesitation; some subtle cowardice perhaps, on the part of the Northern commander. *That* is why he had chosen this audacious course. Splitting his army in the presence of a superior force went against every military rule ever written. It was an almost intangible feeling, but General Lee knew just what the outcome would be if he made his move.

And so it was: The great blue army had suddenly stopped and made ready defensive positions after being pushed ever so slightly by Robert E. Lee's advance guard. Now, the two hosts stood lined up in long rows of infantry and cannons awaiting the upcoming events. A general semi-circle was formed by the much larger Union army, while the Southern army made a conforming arc that stretched their smaller numbers much thinner than their opponents.

The great general turned to his trusted aide, Levy Isaac, as the sun was beginning to set. "Please go fetch me General Jackson, Levy. We must discuss our future plans." he said while smiling kindly at his subordinate.

"Yes sir!" barked Levy as he turned to leave, with his spurs making tinkling sounds as headed for his horse, Sarah.

"Be sure to take care of yourself, Levy. I cannot afford to lose you." the general called out before Levy could mount his horse.

"Of course, sir" he smiled while getting astride his horse and turning in the direction of Stonewall Jackson's headquarters.

As Levy rode through the spring fields, the sun was beginning to dip below the horizon, and a cool breeze began to blow mildly. He realized it was Friday night and his thoughts slipped back to his not-so-distant childhood. A slight pang of guilt edged itself into his consciousness; it was the Jewish Sabbath, and in earlier days he would certainly not have been riding his horse. He would have been at home with his family. His mother would be preparing to light the candles, and the sweet smell of homemade bread would be wafting from the kitchen.

He would head out the door with his father of blessed memory and walk through the paved streets of Richmond on the way to Friday night service at the main Synagogue. His father, as one of the community leaders, would be greeted warmly by everyone as he made his way to the Eastern wall: a place of honor.

"Levy!" the rabbi would exclaim as he walked to his seat. "I'm so glad to see your shining face this Shabbos!"

"Good Shabbos, Rabbi Eisen," would come the reply. "How does the Rav fare?"

"Very well, Levy." He smiled softly and slowly turned toward Levy's father. "Ok, Chaim, you may begin the prayers."

Chaim would ascend to the Bimah[2] and lead the Kabbalt Shabbat[3] service. His sweet melodies would echo from the walls as Levy would be transported into a transcendental, musical world. "Boi V'shalom," Reb Isaac would sing in his top voice as the congregation followed in their prayer books.

The thunder of nearby artillery brought him out of his reverie, and he spurred Sarah on into the darkening night to carry out his mission.

---

[2] The central platform upon which the Torah scroll containing the 5 books of Moses is placed when it is being read to the congregation.
[3] Traditional set of Psalms read before the evening prayers on Friday night.

Chapter Four

Hans and Patrick laughed off the recent attack on their well-being and had moved off in search of a headquarters and orders that would probably get them into exactly what they were looking for: "a whole heap 'o trouble."

Riding into the main camp, they saw all of the trappings of an army in camp and field. Soldiers sat cooking their rations; hard tack and sausage, and if they were lucky, some whiskey. Tents with card playing soldiers in varying degrees of rest and repose greeted their eyes, and the smell of smoke from campfires met their noses as they hurried on towards Hooker's headquarters, which was located in the Chancellorsville mansion.

Captain O'Keefe hurried them in as they arrived. In a low whisper, he spoke stringently. "To the back with you two, and listen carefully to General Hooker!"

Hooker was gesticulating almost wildly. The general looked like the very personification of war. He was tall and erect, with a handsome, clear cut face and piercing blue eyes. His shining buttons shone like the numerous stars on his blue tunic.

"I tell you, the enemy must ingloriously flee before our mighty Army!" He was saying. "Within a fortnight we will be knocking on the door to Richmond! "

A murmur arose from the gathered crowd of generals and lesser officers. Some, like General Couch, had been quite vocal in their protest of the commanding general's decision to halt advance when contact with Lee's army had initially been made. Now, it seemed, to some of those gathered at least, instead of victory, another defeat was at hand.

General Meade was the first to speak out. "General, I say we lay into 'em here and now! If we let them remain where they are, they'll only find some way to attack and surprise us!"

Couch spoke next, "General, if we give them the initiative, we only stand to lose ours, and then they will batter us once again! Do not let us lose! Do not give in to caution!"

Hooker was quick to reply. "I'm positive they are going to withdraw. They can't beat us here, and if they retreat, we've no need to fight them until their backs are turned. That's when we will fight them in the open at the gates of Richmond!" he exclaimed. "The war is almost over and my plans are perfect."

During this heated exchange, a short, rather broad chested and mustachioed officer, with two stars on his shoulders and golden epaulettes, swaggered into the tent and rested against a pole. He seemed to be watching the proceedings with practiced disinterest. His next statements were to have tragic effects for the Union Army and change the course of the war between the states.

As General Hooker ceased speaking, the officer leaning against the pole straightened up and pronounced loudly, "General, I move that we attack them as they retreat! I agree they are fleeing, but why not hit them while they are trying to get away?" As he turned to face the crowd, he smiled as he added, "And we will crush them!"

"Aye, aye. A grand idea, General Sickles! I do believe you have hit the nail on the head! Prepare your troops to pursue the enemy in its flight if your scouts find them." Hooker directed. Then, he turned to the rest. "That is all for now! Return to your troops, and victory on the morrow!"

As everyone was leaving the tent, General Hooker motioned to Captain O'Keefe. "Come here, Captain. I have a special assignment for you and your team, who have proved so capable in the past." He looked a bit nervous now, and sunk his voice to a whisper. "I am not as clear as I seem to be on the movements of our enemies. I must have more information."

He put his hand to his brow and wiped the sweat off that was beginning to bead there. "This is where you come in, Captain O'Keefe. Send your men across enemy lines and bring me that information. A captured soldier would be best."

"Yes, sir!" O'Keefe said as he saluted and eyed Hans and Patrick, who were looking at the floor. They weren't really afraid, but the thought of sure death still shook them both to the core. Despite knowing it was most likely a suicide mission, the excitement and tension began to mount inside them.

Chapter Five

Levy rode into Jackson's camp as night fell. The soldiers were already beginning to light their campfires. The clink of pots and pans and murmuring could be heard; camp sounds. A quick sign and counter sign granted Levy access to the commanding general.

General Jackson was sitting alone by the fire, staring at the embers as they floated skyward. Normally, a general would have been surrounded by a myriad of officers and men vying for his attention, but Stonewall was different. He asked no counsel from others, and divulged his plans to no one, save General Lee, and that was only when asked. He had once commented that, "If my coat knew my plans, I would cast it away."

Levy approached the general, and when he saw that Jackson did not turn to greet him, he cleared his throat.

"Have a seat, lieutenant," murmured the head of the second corps in a half distracted manner, without looking up. "What has General Lee sent you here for?"

"To bring you to him for a council of war."

"Yes, it would seem the time has come to make our plans." Jackson sighed, and then added, "I will be with you in fifteen minutes. Please tell Sergeant Macey to make ready my horse."

As the small party left the camp towards that fateful meeting that would decide the future of thousands of men, Levy couldn't help but feel that history was in the making. Whatever plans would be made, he knew that they would have lasting effects on many lives.

Old Blue Light, a name given to Jackson by his men during the famous Valley Campaign, when the light of battle sprang up in his cold, blue eyes, looked down as his horse trundled along awkwardly under his weight. His grunt was the response after being questioned by one of the party. A strange personality indeed, was this silent, morose leader of men. Deeply religious and moral, he was the very embodiment of an avenging angel on the battlefield; certainly not a favorite of those who opposed him.

Levy's thoughts again floated away towards happier times. His family would sit down for their midday meal on the Sabbath, while his younger sisters would be playing in and around the legs of the long table. A lace white table cloth adorned it, and the best dishes would be laid out as most of his friends would do at their houses for Christmas or Easter. The Levys did this every week. His father would raise the cup in his left hand and recite the ancient blessings over the holiness of the Sabbath and the wine: "Boruch Ata…."

"Levy!" shouted the general's adjutant. "Where has your head got boy? You almost rode into enemy lines! Turn around!"

The young man turned his horse and spurred it back on the path. In the dark, it was so easy to ride off in the wrong direction...

Chapter Six

The jump off point for Hans was somewhere near where Sickles' troops met Couch's. He made his pack ready for the excursion. Basically, he emptied it out, leaving only a bit of hardtack and cured bacon, as well as a blanket. His gun was carried in a holster strapped to his belt, and his knife was sheathed in a small leather scabbard that was tied around his shin; his own invention.

All (well, almost all) of the rest of the party was praying in some way, to some deity. Hans did not believe. He'd seen enough of war and dismemberment, tragedy, and disgrace, to realize that there is no higher power. No all-powerful God had saved the thousands of young men whom he had seen blasted. Blackened faces and glassy eyes looked to the heavens; searching for something they'll never find.

No, he was quite sure that it was all a product of chance; that men, and not God made the present, past, and future what they were. A conviction only enforced by experience. At one point during the battle of Antietam, he'd witnessed a man's throat literally torn out by a Minié ball. He had gasped "I'm killed!" the blood spurting thickly from the wound.

To which his commanding officer replied, "It is merely a scratch! Pick up your gun and move forward!" The man then took a few steps forward and pitched over stone dead.

If men were made in the Lord's image, Han wanted no part of that whole thing. He was Jewish by birth and family, only. He saw in the rituals and traditions of the previous generation only an antiquated mode; a desire to hold onto the past and old superstitions. There was no room in the progressive world of 1863 in which he lived. Fate was the determinate force.

"All ready!" shouted his senior officer. "To your positions! March."

"Here goes," thought Hans, as he trotted to his horse's side. The excitement began to well up inside him again. This was his spirituality. Hans looked over to his friend. Pat gave him a reassuring nod, and they exchanged their brotherly hand shake one more time. Looking away, Hans plunged into the thicket, in search of his quarry.

Chapter Seven

Upon his arrival with the Jackson's party at Lee's camp, Levy was overcome by exhaustion. He could think of nothing else, other than finding a quick repast and a place to bed down for the night. With some pine needles for a pillow, and a horse blanket for warmth, he was soon in a deep slumber. The time was not yet ten pm.

Something woke him from his sleep around midnight or there about. Turning over, he saw two figures about 10 yards away, seated on old cracker boxes in earnest conversation by the fireside. It was impossible to hear more than mumbling and the crackle of the smoldering branches. Before closing his eyes, Levy wondered what these two men, Lee and Jackson, might be discussing. Giving up the mental exercise, he pulled the horse blanket over his head and went back to sleep, leaving the generals to plan what would go down in history as one of the most audacious battle plans of all time.

The bright sun was high in the sky by the time Levy awoke to the nudge of another soldier. "You'd better get moving Levy! General Lee says that you should be his eyes and ears in Old Stonewall's column! They started out yonder already! Catch up quick!"

Wasting no time, Levy shook off the sleep, packed his things, and mounted his horse. Riding along the column was a slow and tedious process. Along the way, he suffered the well-meaning jeers of the infantry marching along. Levy was well recognized by many of the men and they chaffed him good naturedly. "Better get up thar before you catch it for getting behind!" or "Had a good breakfast, sonny?" "Tell Old Jack we're a comin'! Don't let him start the fuss without us!"

For sheer energy and will, there was no army like the Southern army, and in *that* storied army, there were no troops like Stonewall's. They would march until exhausted and fight like demons upon reaching the field. From the looks of it, Fighting Joe was in for it.

Stonewall was in conference with his men as Levy approached. It seemed serious, and four or five men were gathered in earnest conversation at the crossroads. As he caught up with Jackson and his party, he was greeted by a quick salute from Robert Jenkins, a lieutenant on the general's staff.

"What news, Jenkins?" Levy asked.

"They are deciding whether to turn on the Orange Plank Road or continue on their flanking march. It seems like Rhodes is for a more immediate attack while Old Blue Light is for further marching."

Levy always favored a direct approach, but his advice wasn't often heeded, seeing how he was only 21 and a junior Lieutenant.

"I'm for the attack, myself!" Levy exclaimed.

"Yes, well that always means a higher cost in lives." his companion replied. "Anyway, it is not up to us. It is for us to obey our orders from up top."

As they were finishing their conversation, a horseman galloped by and reigned up in front of the group of senior commanders at the crossroads. With his horse all frothy from exertion, he leaped off and ran the last few feet to where Jackson was.

"They are attacking us from behind!" came the report. "A whole corps or more rushed out and is threatening to split us from the main army!"

A look of stone set on the General's impassive face. A moment like this was a crisis in any man's life, and the decision made here might cost the South the war. Two and a half years of bloodshed and struggle all for naught if the wrong steps were made now.

"We move on our intended course! Continue the flanking march." he said quietly, his voice just above a whisper.

General Rhodes nodded, and then turned to his assistant and mumbled a few commands. The junior officer quickly faced about and headed off in the direction of the column to give instructions.

The captain's voice broke in over the inflight speaker system. "Uh, we seem to be hitting some more turbulence, folks. I'm going to put on the fasten seatbelt sign because things might get a bit bumpy."

The fasten seat belt sign turned on again, and Aaron sat back down in his seat and buckled his safety harness. Until now, and for the past hour or so, he had been telling the tale of the prayer book to his traveling companion who had loosened his demeanor considerably.

"Aaron," they were now on a first name basis. "I'm loving the whole war story but where does that Siddur come into all of this?"

"That's what I was getting to before I was rudely interrupted by the fasten seatbelt sign and the announcement from the captain."

The plane was beginning to shimmy and shake considerably, and drinks were sliding off tray tables. A worried look could be seen on a few faces, but the stewardess showed no signs of concern, so Aaron was relaxed and smiled as he prepared to continue the story.

Avi gave a quick glance at the siddur in Aaron's hand and swallowed hard. He didn't exactly like flying. "I hope you prayed well before…"

An even broader smile creased Aaron's handsome face. "I thought you didn't believe in this 'stuff,' Avi"

"Keep moving with the story," he said, clearly embarrassed by his little slip.

Chapter Eight

"Levy, come here please! I have an assignment for you that I think will be to your liking. It will be dangerous. Are you up for it?"

It was rare to be addressed by General Jackson at all, and even rarer still to be asked if one would like an assignment. Usually it was an order.

"Yes sir! I will do as commanded" Levy straightened himself up proudly while saluting.

"Come with me to the side then."

"Levy, this is what I need you to do," Jackson stated as he turned away from the group while leading Levy by the shoulder. "General Lee needs to know that we have been attacked in the rear. You have to make contact with the rest of the army at Chancellorsville and let them know we will continue on our flanking march to come up in the rear of the Army of the Potomac! We shall catch them unawares, as they will not be expecting us! Your task will be extremely dangerous, as you must cross enemy lines in search of our own. If you are caught, you may jeopardize the entire mission! Do not let yourself be captured! Are all of my instructions clear?"

"Yes sir!" Levy barked. His heart had dropped into his stomach upon hearing the assignment but he was not about to refuse it now after accepting it initially. "I understand very well what is wanted of me and will carry it out to the letter, Sir!"

Deep in the thicket, about 2 linear miles away, Hans, his face darkened by ashes, had already embarked on his mission, completely unaware of the events about to transpire. Bright sunlight streamed in through the branches overhead, and a small stream flowed past his well-chosen hiding spot. He couldn't hear a single bird's chirping, as they had all already flown from the battleground. The distant chatter of small arms fire and the crumph of mortars interrupted the tranquil scene.

Lying in wait amongst the brambles brought with it the thrill of the hunt. His unexpecting prey would walk or ride by, completely unaware of his presence. Hans loved this part. Fierce energy welled up inside him as he readied himself to pounce. The only irksome part was having to remain perfectly still, lest a rustle of leaves or twitch of branches give him away.

Hark! Hans' head swiveled quickly to better command the view to his right. A horse and rider cautiously picked their way through the brush. Looking around, the rider seemed to breathe a sigh of relief upon finding himself alone. The soldier perched atop the steed was not more than twenty years old, and was very slight in build; almost girlish. Outfitted in a gray uniform that looked like it had just been taken from the tailor, he dismounted to let his horse drink from the gurgling stream.

Levy was nervous knowing full well that the enemy was all around him. He had but a thousand yards to go and he would be inside the Southern lines. Those thousand yards had to be crossed without cover. Tall grass and gently rolling fields were no place for a lone soldier, especially on horseback. The smoke from random shots showed that the pickets were still active. He could lead his horse and use her for cover. Not a great option unless you wanted to become part of the scenery. Better to let the action die down and then move.

Levy's boots were eye level with Hans now. Calculating the perfect time to take his captive, Hans rose silently while removing the knife from its sheath...

Suddenly, Levy felt a cold, leather glove cover his mouth. Simultaneously, a gigantic clasp knife was thrust against his neck. He felt the cold steel pressed so hard and close that he was given the impression that just breathing would bring it all to an end. Beads of sweat broke out on his forehead as he willed himself to call out for help.

In response, more to his thought than deed, Levy's captor hissed in his ear. "One peep out of you, Johnny Reb and I'll slice you open like the pig you are! Now, blink twice if you understand me!"

Levy obliged, seeing no other choice presenting itself. This apparition who had grabbed him from behind seemed earnest in his intentions.

"OK, that's a good boy. I'm gonna take my hand from your mouth. If you call out, so help me, I'll bury my knife to the hilt in your worthless carcass! Blink twice if you heard me!"

Levy hesitated.

"Blink Dammit, or I'll be as good as my word!"

The blade pressed harder against Levy's flesh.

He blinked twice. The pressure eased slightly and the glove was removed from his face.

"Stop! Now, don't turn around boy! Move real slow towards your horse! "Hans spoke with his upstate New York accent heavily apparent when he was excited as he was now. The "O" in "Stop" almost sounded like an "A".

"When you get to the horse I want you grab the reins with both hands. Easy now! Easy!"

Hans had to figure out how to get his captive back behind his lines, but he needed time to think, and having his charge keep his hands where he could see them gave him a chance to relax a bit. Gave him time to make up his mind.

Levy, for his part, was happy to have the knife removed from his neck. He couldn't scream, else this Northern heathen would likely make his mamma one sad lady. Best to stay still and try to make a break when his captor was distracted.

Hans didn't have to wait long for his chance to spirit away his prize. A sudden *hurrah* sounded from the woods across the field as a Union cavalry charge erupted from the brush. Sabers swinging and pistols drawn, they charged obliquely into a line of grey infantry arrayed against the main Northern line in that sector. The Rebel Yell rose shrill and intense and could be heard in stark contrast to the deep throated cheer of the Blue Cavalry. As the fighting grew in intensity, all eyes were rooted to the action at hand. Little heed was given to the small party quickly making their way across the now empty field in the direction of Sickles' Headquarters.

A shout rose from the Southern side as someone there turned and spotted the horse and the two fugitives. A few shots rang out, which pattered among the tall grass as Hans pushed and prodded Levy forward. Then, the firing stopped as the soldiers turned towards more urgent matters. Who cared about a few stragglers when the full weight of the opposing army was being pressed against them?

Safe within his own lines, Hans pulled his pistol from his belt and pointed it in Levy's direction.

"Hands where I can see 'em!" he shouted. "He's my prisoner, it's all right," this to a group of blue infantry who appeared on the scene. "I've got him well in hand." He turned to his captive again, "Now, sit down!"

Again, with little choice but to obey, Levy lowered himself to the ground all the while staring at his tormentor with unhidden fury in his eyes.

"Name and rank, junior." Hans demanded.

"I'll be damned if I give you the courtesy!" Levy snarled.

"What did you say? I missed that. Name and rank!" Hans exclaimed, cocking the wicked looking six shooter in his hand.

"I knew you Northern boys were dumb but I didn't know you were deaf as well. I said I'll be damned if I give you the courtesy!"

This Southern boy didn't seem too scared, especially considering his present position. Hans admired that. He would have to try a different tack, but first he had to get his prisoner into headquarters so he would be able to interrogate him.

"Okay, Mr. Be Damned. Let's get you checked in." Hans said with a mischievous grin. "Move it!"

Hans smacked his captive lightly across the head with his gun after seeing the indignant expression looking up at him. "Move, you piece of trash!"

Chapter Nine

As Hans marched Levy through the Union camp, looks and stares were the order of the day. A few choice curses exited more than one mouth as well. The Northern boys were not too keen on their southern brethren.

General Sickles was to be found outside of his tent, standing tall on both legs; one of which was to be lost in the great battle of Gettysburg only three months hence. Couriers were running to and from the general bearing news from all quarters, informing him of progress and regress as the case was.

As Hans thrust a manacled Levy in front of the chief, Sickles turned in his direction.

"Well, who is this man?"

"Sir, I've brought this captive in from the enemy lines!" Hans barked.

"Excellent work! Please get his information recorded and we shall have a little chat with him as soon as I am able to make the time."

'Yessir!" came the salute.

Inside the tent, Levy was pushed into a camp chair and trussed with a spare rope a little more roughly than might have been warranted. "Animal!" he exclaimed.

"Well, my butternut clad friend, are you ready to give me your name and rank?" Hans said, ignoring the remark.

"Not you or any man can make me tell you anything! I shan't disclose anything and I'll keep my mouth shut. Do what you will!" Levy said defiantly; almost like a stubborn child refusing his chores.

"Fair enough, boy. I'll just take the liberty of searching your saddle bag." Hans leaned over and began rummaging through the brown leather pouch.

Straining on his bonds, Levy grunted through clenched teeth. "You heathen! Put it down!"

"What are you afraid I'll find? Hmmmm?" Hans sneered.

"Put it down!" Levy shouted loud enough for everyone outside the tent to hear, despite the din of battle.

"OK. OK. Lets' see," Hans said ignoring the protest. "Hmm, some corn bread, dried beef, a knife, blanket, and... What's this?"

Hans lifted a rather thick book from the pouch and held it up. It was about the size of one of those music boxes Hans had seen on his trip to New York City some time back. Inscribed with cryptic writing on its front and side, he could make neither heads nor tails of it.

Levy, meanwhile could restrain himself no longer, and kicking and screaming, toppled himself over while still strapped to the chair; all the while screaming, "Put it back in my bag! Put my Siddur down!"

"Your what?" a puzzled Hans asked, not quite knowing what the big deal was. Here was this book with the strange writing on it and there was a very upset boy soldier pleading him to put it back in the bag. He also called it a "Siddur." Odd indeed. Truth be told, Hans had seen these letters before, way back one time when he was at his Grandma's house.

Just then, a contingent of soldiers burst into the tent. They were Hans' fellow spies.

"Waddya got here, Hans?" one of them asked. "A Reb!"

Hans shrugged, "He won't talk and he ain't got anything here to tell me much about him."

"What's that you're holding in your hands?" someone else asked.

"Give it here, Hans." another shouted. "Let's see what this rebel scum is getting all flustered about!"

Hans looked at his charge, who was now mumbling quietly to himself on his side, still tied to the chair, with his back to Hans and his comrades. He looked back at his fellow soldiers.

"It's nothing," he said as he stuffed the book back in the bag. Levy stopped murmuring and looked up at Hans thankfully.

"Nothing important." Hans spake, and then changed the subject. "Where's Pat?"

The other soldiers looked at the floor, none saying a word, but looking mighty uncomfortable.

"Where is Pat?" Hans' voice began to rise. "Come out with it!"

Finally, someone spoke up. "Pat's in the hospital tent, Hans. He was um," he couldn't get it out. "He was shot a few hours before we were able to get back here. Some Rebs ambushed him as he was getting on his horse. We took them out, but there was nothing we could do for Pat; he was shot in the gut. Jenkins tried to dress the wound and clean it, but it just looks really bad, right Jenkins?"

Jenkins just nodded, feeling immense sympathy for Hans right about now.

Hans hung his head in disbelief. "Where is he? Which tent?" Hans needed to see his friend. In the two short years he had spent in the war, most of it had been with Patrick. Marching together, fighting, and generally having a great time; they had been inseparable, but now...

Without saying so much as a word, Jenkins stepped out and pointed toward a small, feeble canvas tent that had a white flag with a red cross on it, which was moving imperceptibly in the gentle breeze. A tear welled up in Hans' eyes as the thought rushed through his veins. As he turned his back to his prisoner, he made a declaration. "I'm going to say goodbye to my friend. Leave this man until I get back to speak with him first." The troops dared not argue with him and nodded in agreement.

With that, the troops left the tent in a group. Hans pressed his hands to his head and stifled a cry. Levy watched him quietly as he walked out of the tent wiping his eyes. Ten minutes ago, the prisoner feared and held hatred for his captor; now, he felt nothing but trust and sympathy towards Hans.

As he trounced through the dirt and made his way to the hospital tent, Hans fought to hide his sorrow. He lifted the tent and peered in. What he saw cracked his heart right down the center. A doctor looked up at him and shook his head, silently breaking the news to Hans. He got up and left the two friends alone for one last time.

Pat's body was all but covered in blood. His hands lay crossed over his midsection, where a deep wound marked the spot where the fatal bullet had struck. Hans dropped to his knees and held his friend's hands with his own. His head fell and sobs were held back as tightly as they could be. Suddenly, Pat's voice rang out, "I got the one that shot me."

Hans looked up, disbelieving of what he just heard. Pat's eyes looked back at him, and he managed a half-hearted smile. "Don't be crying just yet, man. Give them something to cry about first." Hans smiled and gripped Pat's hands even tighter.

"It's gonna be a lot less enjoyable without you next to me." His voice almost broke under the emotional weight of his words. Pat looked back at him before slowly closing his eyes. Hans waited for his response, but it never came. His hands began to grow cold, and that's when he knew his friend was no longer fighting for the Union with him.

A single tear dropped from his eyes as he bid his friend goodbye. He rose to his feet, wiped at his cheeks, and marched out of that tent with new determination. Time to give the Confederacy a reason to feel this kind of pain.

"Name's Levy. I'm a lieutenant on Lee's staff," intoned the Southerner as Hans walked back into his tent. "I really appreciate what you did back there, saving my Siddur and all. I figure my name's the least I can give you."

Hans turned and wiped a tear from his eye. "It's nothing, really. I saw one of these books before. It's a prayer book of sorts, correct?" He needed to change the topic so his mind wouldn't be lost in his despair.

"Yes it is. That book has prayers in it that are almost 1900 years old! Our Torah and those prayers have been a sustaining force for my people for thousands of years!"

"Those are my people, too!" Hans cried emphatically. "I didn't know I captured a fellow Hebrew. What are the odds?"

It was Levy's turn to be shocked. "You're a what?"

Hans certainly didn't look the traditional part, with his blue eyes and sharp nose. "A Jew. You have wax in your Rebel ears?"

Chuckling slightly, Levy mumbled, "Behold, the Lord neither sleeps nor slumbers. Always on the lookout. What are the chances?"

The camaraderie he felt with this newfound member of the clan must have made him drop his guard. Before he knew what he was doing, he blurted out, "I'm sure glad I'm not in your General's shoes when old Jackson falls on his flank and rear."

It was like a lightning bolt! Hans realized the import of the information he had just heard. This could change the battle drastically and even cost the North the war! "Our what and what? That's important information, my fine Rebel friend! You'll have to be processed at headquarters right away, and I've got to warn a certain General, so let's go! Up with you! Out!"

Chapter Ten

As the smoke from the distant lines drifted skyward, General Hooker glanced at his maps, and then back across the fields. Pacing the porch of the Chancellorsville Mansion, which he had recently made his headquarters, distractedly, he thought, "What did it all mean?" The Rebels should have been in full retreat by now if his previous surmise had been correct. Why were they still there, and why did his scouts bring him no information as to their movements? Very frustrating.

He had been to see the right flank, and General Howard had given him a tour of his battle lines. He got to see all the troops huddled together in unison. "How strong! How strong!" Hooker had proclaimed at the time, but he wasn't quite sure as this part of the entrenchments were "in the air," that is, they rested on no natural obstacles and could therefore be assaulted in flank and rear should the enemy show up there. Some niggling details just seemed wrong, although he couldn't put his finger on the precise problem.

Because of this, he had offered to send a brigade of two to shore up the lines, but had not protested when Howard refused the help. Now, his conscience bothered him mightily. Above the constant patter of picket fire and artillery thumps, he suddenly heard some shouting and the sound of horses galloping up a dirt road. From the lines in front, two horses dashed toward him, the second with two riders. The passenger was bedecked in Confederate gray, manacled, and looking none too happy at his current circumstance.

Captain O'Keefe leapt off his horse and bounded up the steps to the porch where the General was standing. "General!" he barked and hastily saluted. "We've captured a Rebel with important information. He let slip about something huge!"

"Nice work! Well Captain, inside with you and your party. Let's hear what you've learned."

Hans climbed down from his horse and pulled Levy down after him, shoving him into the parlor. The look that Levy wore on his face was the most stoic expression he could manage. Truth be told, he was quaking in his boots after blurting out the Confederate position back there in the tent. Now, everything was at stake and the General of the entire Union army was about to question him. His slip could spell the end of the Rebel Forces and by extension, the Rebel Cause. If their flanking movement was checked, Hooker could send his reserves swarming over the trenches in his front, knowing full well that they would be lightly populated. General Lee had divided his army twice in the face of a numerically superior foe and he didn't have

23

enough men to man his defenses properly.

After being ushered into the parlor that served as headquarters in the home, with its adjacent fields and crossroads, comprised Chancellorsville, Captain O'Keefe roughly pushed Levy towards a chair against the wall. Hooker had left to summon his staff clerk so as to record the information about to be extracted from the captive.

"Sit down there, Rebel and not a word if you know what's good for you! You'll talk when the General returns." O'Keefe grumbled as he tested the ropes holding Levy's hands.

"Now, Hans please be as clear as possible when you explain to the general what you heard from this here boy-soldier." the captain spoke while nodding towards the prisoner.

"Yes, sir!"

The sound of boots on wood flooring was heard coming from the hall, and in stepped Hooker, along with his clerk and a few other staff officers who were trying to look important.

"Hans, my boy! Great work!" Hooker smiled warmly as he wrapped his arms around the young soldier. He then turned to Captain O'Keefe, "Tell us this important news learned because of his heroic exploits."

"Well sir, this rebel Hans captured," he said, while pointing at Levy, "let slip that the whole Rebel Army is en route around the right flank of our army! To what purpose, we can only guess."

Hooker's face became ashen for a split second, and then resumed its ruddy hue.

"It seems impossible! A ruse like that is not likely. They are in full retreat. Sure, didn't General Sickles prove it today with his foray?"

Captain O'Keefe glanced at Hans, who had kept his gaze fixed on the General the entire time. If the captain was looking for a sign that his subordinate was making something up, he wouldn't find it.

One of Hooker's staff spoke up, "General, Okeefe's men have never given misinformation. As wild as the idea seems, it is Lee and Jackson we are contending with. We all remember what happened at the Second Bull Run. No one expected them to show up on our right, but there they were."

The General stepped to the door and looked out. Contemplating the situation, his hand flew instinctively to the wound which he had gained on the field of Antietam.

"True, true..." grumbled Hooker. "But I still can't believe it. Doesn't fit with anything we've observed. The Rebels are fleeing and they hold their trenches with a token force. By George, I should order an attack right now!"

Thinking better of it, the General unclenched his fist and turned around, looking each of the group in the eye. Everyone except for Hans cast their gaze at the floor.

General Hooker continued, "Let us see for ourselves what our prisoner has to say."

Levy felt every eye upon him and chose the safest course. He lied. A big, bold-faced lie: a fabrication that in any other situation but this would have made him laugh.

"General, I have told an untruth. When this heathen," Levy indicated Hans but jutting out his elbow toward him. "When this heathen captured me and held a gun to my head, I told him what I thought he wanted to hear: That we were going to attack, so that he would tell everyone he met what I told him, and thus give our army a chance to retreat. It was for this reason I was sent by General Jackson in the first place. I was to report to General Lee as to our progress with the retreat. We were to get a lead on the Union army and then form the blocking force for the retreat of the rest of our army!"

A general murmur of assent erupted from those gathered. The only one who seemed to be unaffected by Levy's speech was Hans. He cocked his head in a curious fashion and didn't remove his gaze from the prisoner.

"General!" Hans shouted, "He's lying! I can tell right away! What he told me in the tent was the truth. When I saved his..." At this point Hans stopped, not wanting to have Levy's prayer book become the subject of an investigation. "When I saved him from being pistol whipped, he blurted out what the Rebs were really planning!"'

The commander looked thoughtful for a moment.

"Hmmmm, I wonder," the General spoke more to himself than those present.

Hans continued with emphasis, "The Rebs are forming on our flank sure as I'm standing here, General! I know it, and if you'll let me prove it, well..."

Hooker cut him off with a wave of his hand. "Lieutenant, I understand your concerns, but all of our information points the other way. Wouldn't you agree, Captain O'Keefe?"

O'Keefe, finding himself in the uncomfortable position of having to choose between supporting one of his men or agreeing with the chief commander, chose the latter course.

He nodded and then spoke. "I believe this scout is a plant by the Southern Army. He is meant to distract us to a point where we lose sight of him in his retreat. None of my other men have given over such information." As he turned, he gave Hans a knowing look, with a hint of sorrow in his eyes. He was trying to convey his apology without saying it outright.

Hans looked angrily from his commander to the chief. "General! This is all wrong. I cannot stand by while we are ambushed!"

O'Keefe now lost his temper. "Lieutenant. You will stand down! Your input is no longer asked for at this point! You will do as ordered."

"Yes, sir." mumbled Hans, who seemed far from satisfied.

Chapter Eleven

The seatbelt sign went on once again. Avi sighed and sat down in his seat, performing the buckle-up ritual once again. The constant turbulence made Avi nervous, but Aaron seemed unperturbed. The story was getting exciting and his own Scheherazade, no relation, kept getting interrupted by that blinking light.

Sweating a bit, Avi looked at the Siddur in Aaron's hand once more. "Can you explain again what that prayer is all about?"

"Why Avi, I never thought you'd ask!" Aaron grinned. "Of course. I'm sure you can translate the words, but the meaning is basically asking Hashem to guard us on our travels and protect us from the common dangers involved with such. Very comforting to know that someone much more powerful than we are, is in charge."

Upon completing his sentence, Aaron glanced at the stewardess again, who, for the first time, seemed a bit nervous. This certainly was a turbulent flight. Children were nervously grabbing the arms of their parents. The looks of concern were hard to miss on crew and passenger alike.

Then, the immense, consistent turbulence was brought to an abrupt pause when the shaking suddenly ceased.

Avi turned to his traveling companion and clucked his tongue while issuing forth the universal Israeli sign of impatience: "Nu?"

"How did that Siddur get into your whole story? I'm still not seeing the connection."

"You'll see soon enough, chaver." Aaron cracked his knuckles and resumed his narrative with great relish. "We rejoin our two heroes outside of the Chancellorsville mansion…"

O'Keefe was yelling at Hans, "Where in the name of all that is holy do you think you're headed?!"

Hans turned on his heel and pushed his face right up to his commanding officer's steaming countenance. "I know there's about to be an avalanche of Rebs coming straight down on our flank. I can't just do nothing. This Confederate scout lied to General Hooker! I know it, and I'm bringing him to General Howard to prove it!"

Levy, for his part, was trying to be as inconspicuous as possible. Not an easy thing to do when Hans poked him repeatedly in the chest for emphasis during this heated exchange.

O'Keefe was beside himself. Unaccustomed to being spoken to in this fashion, he wasn't quite sure how to respond. He chose anger as the most reliable option.

"I promise you, Hans that if you disobey the General's orders I'll have you thrown in the pen 'till we can arrange a proper court martial!"

"That's if you can catch me!" and with that, Hans ran for his horse, dragging Levy behind him. Reaching his mount, he pushed his captive up and then leaped up himself. With one final glance at O'Keefe, he spurred his horse towards the right flank of the Union Army, and history.

O'Keefe had time to mumble, "I hope you know what you're doing, Hans." before turning to address Hooker and the knot of officers who had gathered on the porch when the commotion had first erupted.

Riding at breakneck pace, Hans expertly guided his horse over and through the many ravines and undulations that marked the landscape. Through a copse of trees and bursting into the sunlight again, he couldn't help but think of his time spent as a youth herding his grandfather's cattle in upstate New York.

Each summer, he would leave the sultry heat of the city of Rochester for the old farm about forty miles inland from Ontario. There, he would spend his days working the farm and riding for pleasure. Ah, the mere thought calmed him. It seemed a far cry from the heat of battle, with its screaming missiles and groaning soldiers in various states of injury as the very air was alive with the hum of a thousand bullets.

Yet, those memories also brought him back to a bitter place; a place where the mere fact he was Jewish meant torture and persecution at the hands of his schoolmates. The worst part was, he was dealt even darker deeds at the hands of his teachers, and those experiences made him yearn to be free: free of religion, free of prejudice, and free of the confines imposed on him for being born a member of the Hebrew tribe. Spending a day locked in a shed on a sweaty June day by the headmaster for refusing to acknowledge a god your forefathers didn't worship will do that to a person. Hans wanted to be as far from Judaism as possible, and here he was riding with a professed practitioner of the religion. God did, if nothing else, possess of a fine sense of humor.

Levy was scared witless. Not so much of the incredibly fast ride, but of the unknown intentions of the man steering the horse. Despite the recent evidence to the contrary, this Yankee spy might just dump him in a ditch or worse once he had fulfilled his purpose. Not exactly the best way to end the day. His mind raced for a way out--some solution to the problem of escape, but none presented itself. Best just to hang on for the ride and act as circumstances dictated.

The rough ride came to an abrupt end once the pair reached Howard's lines, which seemed surprisingly tranquil. Soldiers carried their plates to cook and returned to consume their meal beside their tents or otherwise rested, relaxed, played cards, and so forth. A few sentries marched up and back, in front of the long line of encampments

The whole appearance was more of the camp Hans had been in when McClellan was preparing for his ill-fated Peninsula campaign: preparing, training, and regrouping, more so than that of an army corps on the frontlines during a major battle. No matter. Hans had a mission to fulfill and he wasn't going to let some lax commander's misjudgments get in the way of his saving the army from a well prepared sneak assault by the wily Jackson.

Looking down at his pocket watch, Hans saw it was 4:45. The assault couldn't be delayed much longer, or darkness would ruin the chances of success. Therefore, he had to hurry! Where was the headquarters tent? Where was Howard? He had to find him.

Chapter Twelve

General Howard stepped out of his headquarters at Dowdall's Tavern and puffed up his chest. It had been a long, hard climb, but he was now the head of a corps in the great Army of the Potomac. A leader of nearly 12,000 men, and he was just in his 33rd year. True, he'd left an arm on the battlefield at Fair Oaks, but it was a small price to pay for his current position.

"How strong! How strong!" he echoed his commander's words in referring to his lines. Hooker had exclaimed the same thing and Howard thought it a testimony to his capability.

Yet, he had to temper his pride. Arrogance, after all, was against his very religious beliefs. He was a staunch Christian and put his faith in God in all his decision making. He was just about to have his faith tested.

Without even an inkling of the Confederate avalanche about to descend on his flank and rear, Howard imagined himself leading his corps in a triumphant pursuit of the Rebel army. He would bring the sword of justice to bear on this rabble who convulsed the country with their silly defense of states' rights and that "curious institution"[4] that had no place in a modern nation like the United States of America in 1863!

"General! General!" the shout came from his left. His aide, O'Hara, was the source. A dusty soldier dragging a young confederate soldier was right behind. Howard turned to face the words.

"General," said O'Hara panting "this soldier here claims to have important information! He says our corps is in serious danger!"

"Nonsense!" Howard started to shout, but then his better judgment caught him by the throat. "Well, what of his information?" he said in surly fashion.

"He says the Rebs are about to ambush us! They're in those woods as we speak!" he exclaimed, pointing to the trees. "A whole corps of 'em!"

Howard had the chill of imminent doom grab his heart momentarily. The next second, he had shaken it off. "I'm inclined to disbelieve him, but... let's hear his testimony, then."

O'Hara nodded towards Hans, giving him the floor, or dirt patch, as the case was.

"Sir!" Hans energetically began. "This Rebel captive here let slip that Jackson has lead his entire corps around our flank! If we don't rearrange our position to meet him, we'll be completely railroaded!"

---

[4] Popular euphemism for the practice of slavery at the time.

Howard opened his mouth to answer this audacious outburst, but was cut short by the patter of the feet of a thousand or more woodland creatures running through and past the eleventh corps' tents. These of course had been chased from their homes by nearly twenty thousand pairs of legs belonging to Jackson's men, who at that moment were seconds away from crashing into the unexpecting Union forces.

The first blue troops to react were the dazed sentries who had been told by their superiors that there was nothing more dangerous than a rogue coyote in the woods in front.

Private Perkins' eyes widened when the hint of butternut uniform and flashing steel broke the green canopy. He had just enough time to turn and yell, "The Rebs are coming!" before he was shot down; the barrage nearly tearing his body apart.

Now, bullets and bayonets came from all directions as the Union forces were enveloped flank and rear by the surprise attack so skillfully planned that an entire army was caught unawares.

A perfect stampede of the right side of the blue army began with veteran soldiers running for their lives in the general opposite direction of their tormentors.

Back at the headquarters tent, Howard had rushed inside at the sound of the first shots and emerged with his sword. He then hurried off in the direction of his horse. O'keefe had done the same, leaving Hans and Levy in utter astonishment. The next moment, as if by mutual accord, they ran together towards a ditch that was half completed. Diving in just in time, the tramp of hundreds of boots shook the ground over their heads, and the brigades rushed past.

A Rebel soldier fell in the fissure and Hans reached out with his knife. A shriek of pain, and the unknown soldier was out of the hole again to resume the pursuit.

"Just nicked him! An inch more and he'd have been done for."

"Lucky for him!"

Hans merely nodded and resumed his defensive crouch.

Chapter Thirteen

As the sun set, the ditch became engulfed in shadow. The din of battle had passed the spot where Hans and Levy sat concealed. Southern accents could be heard now and again, but the clipped tones of the Northerner wafted towards their position as well, which told them how the cards lay. They were in between the two lines. A most dangerous place. If they were discovered by either side, they'd be made quick work of.

"You idiot!" Levy hissed between clenched teeth. "You thought you'd save your army? You thought you'd be a hero, and here you've gotten us stuck in this ditch! What were you thinking? "

Hans responded calmly, given the current situation. "There's no use in getting your bonnet in a bunch. I could just shoot you and be off at nightfall and take my chances, or we could work together to get out of this hole. Up to you."

"Fine!" Levy huffed, seeing Hans' side of the argument. "Well, what's your plan then?"

"Not sure. Hasn't come to me yet. When I think it up, you'll be the first to know."

Levy considered. "If it's all the same to you, I'll just say some Tehilim. Hashem will help us."

"Some what?"

"Tehilim. You know, Psalms?"

"I've heard some of that done by the older ladies when they're nervous, but I've never seen a youngster like yourself involved. Those old superstitions are just hogwash, if you ask me."

"Whether you believe it or not, these words we say have been with the Jewish people for nearly two thousand years. In times of trouble, Tehilim, or Pslams as you know them, are the one solid thing you can always count on. Here now, listen to this verse:"

Hans rolled his eyes, but didn't exactly turn away either. Let's listen he thought, then I'll pass judgement.

"'Hinei Mah Tov UManayim. Shevas Achim Gam Yachad.' translates as 'Behold what is good and pleasant'" Levy began, "brothers sitting as one."

"Now that sounds nice. Maybe if we could 'sit as one,' then this whole blasted war wouldn't have started. I like that"

"You really think so? I'm not so sure we're all brothers to begin with. But if we were, then sitting together would indeed be pleasant and nice."

"Yes, I do think that. I feel that you people are wrong! Remember how you got mad at me before for trying to be a hero? Maybe it's the same thing with this whole rebellion! The South is trying to be some hero, and they'll pay. Pay dearly for the effort, they will!"

As Hans was ending his political soliloquy, a screaming shell dropped in between them both. This was no ordinary cannonball, but what was known as a canister. Essentially, it was a tin can full of leaden balls. This tried-and-true piece of weaponry was extremely effective at mowing down troops by the score. After exploding, it would send its seeds of destruction, lead balls usually, in all directions. This very device had found its way into the hole Hans and Levy shared.

Worse yet, it was still smoking. Seconds away from exploding and mustering both of them out of their regiments permanently, it fizzled at the fuse and lay still. Levy froze with a look of terror on his youthful face. His companion had no such reaction. Hans jumped forward and heaved the projectile out of their ditch. A great explosion shook the trench and dirt showered in, along with a good deal of smoke.

Coughing, Hans returned to his place, panting as if he'd run a marathon. Sweat trickled down his neck and made him uncomfortable. He enjoyed thrills, but that was too close for comfort.

Levy sat lost in thought for some time and then said, "Hans, can I trouble you for my siddur? There's something in it that our current situation made me think of."

Hans handed the book to him with a look of curiosity on his face. What in this ancient text could possibly relate to their present condition?

"You see this line?" Levy pointed with a dusty finger. "It says blessed are thou God, Lord of the Universe, Shield of Abraham."

Hans was starting to catch on. The dark room of his mind, where most questions of spirituality were kept, lit up as if someone had struck a match. It was all starting to come together.

"Hashem is our shield! Two children of Abraham shielded by God Almighty!" Levy continued. "You see how clear it is?"

Hans nodded thoughtfully. "Well, let's see how strong the shield is because it will take a lot more than an old blessing to see us through this!"

"He will Hans, He will. I feel it."

Chapter Fourteen

Night fell and the cold set in. It was cool for May. Levy, shivering, looked up at the clear sky. From the trench, it was like looking up from the bottom of a well, with stars shining like jewels on a black velvet setting. If it wasn't for the war erupting over his head, this would be one of the most peaceful visions he'd ever experienced.

"Ma Rabo Masecha!" he exclaimed. "How great are your works, Hashem!"

Hans cocked an eye at Levy. "You've got a Hebrew saying for everything it seems." Then, with a touch of exasperation in his voice, "and how can you praise God when we're stuck in this mud hole?" he made a sweeping gesture and continued, "with almost no chance of getting out alive!"

"I guess you can attribute it to my upbringing," Levy answered. "But, look up and tell me that some human hand fashioned that!" he said pointing skyward. "Impossible!"

"Might be, I'll admit it, but who says God is still there directing things? Seems like people do whatever they want to. They make wars and kill whenever the urge strikes them."

"Judaism teaches us that we have free will. We can do what we want up to a certain point."

"Now that doesn't make any sense!" Hans stated emphatically. "How can God direct things AND give people free will? Now, I'm no professor, but that right there is a contradiction if ever I heard one!"

"You have the choice, but if you make the wrong one then someone else will make the right one. Whatever Hashem wants history to be, that's what it will be. You choose which side you're on, the good or the bad."

"I guess, but it still doesn't seem right--all this suffering" Hans sighed.

"No, I can't say that it does, but we have to have *bitachon*; trust. If you look at our history, Jewish history, you'd see the providence in it all. "

Hans had had enough of this discussion. All the intellectualizing was making his head hurt. He switched topics.

"What was it like growing up religious and all?"

"Beautiful! I still think about going to shul with my father on Friday nights. The singing and the warmth are still with me, even now. Shabbos is a wonder! You cannot work, but must desist from all work. It is a time for study and being with family."

"So, no work? Like a day off? I could always use one of those!"

"No, not that kind of work. More like, no lighting fires or riding a horse."

"What does that have to do with work? It's just living. What happens if you get cold? You can't light a fire?"

"No, you can't, but you can get a blanket!" Levy grinned. "Work is defined by the Bible as anything that was done to build the *Mishkan* or Tabernacle when the Jews were in the desert. It says there are 39 types of work we can't do, and lighting a fire is one of them. There's also cutting wheat, carrying, and many others."

"Humph! Ancient traditions maybe, but that ain't work!"

"Who says you know what work is? Maybe work is defined differently than society says it is. Maybe work is about creating."

"OK, I never thought about it that way. Interesting."

Levy was about to say something exceedingly profound, or at least he hoped it would be, when the sound of horses' hooves broke in on their hushed conversation. From the sound of it, it was a miniscule party of officers. If it was regular cavalry, the talk would be boisterous, if subdued. Instead, they spoke in low tones about serious matters.

Levy covered his head with his arms and prayed hard.

Hans tensed as he listened to their talk. Adjusting his position slightly and gripping the pistol in his holster, he prepared to defend himself from whatever may be coming across their hiding spot. Twisting, he drew his weapon and rose to the edge of the pit, firing off two quick shots. A yell, more yells, and the sound of shuffling hooves told of the havoc wreaked by the barrage just sent forth.

"Back down the trail!" they heard one of the party shout.

Another exclaimed, "Get the General behind our lines!"

Hans quickly ducked back into the hole with a look of amusement on his face. "Gave them something to think about," he whispered to Levy.

"Were they gray or blue?"

"Not sure, Confederate I think."

Just then, a roll of small-arms fire erupted from the near woods. More yelling, and neighing of the horses, and then more gunfire.

Suddenly, someone screamed above the din, "General Jackson is with us! Check your fire!"

"The general is hit!"

Hans and Levy sat captivated by the events occurring above. Was it true? Had General Jackson been in that knot of officers? If so, Hans had just forced them into an ambuscade with his shots, and now it seemed the most feared Southern general was down!

More scuffling and screams brought more soldiers to the scene.

Hans and Levy peeked above the rim together. They saw a group of soldiers gathered around the general: some of them kneeling, others calling for help. Finally, the general was hoisted across a horse's back and led back toward the Confederate lines. Barely able to raise his head, the general lay limp with his left arm tied to his body. Blood was splattered across his face and a look of resignation was the main emotion on his sharp features.

As he was being led away, a spattering of shots was directed at the group from across the field. They moved quickly now, standing between the general and the new assault with their horses and bodies. One of them looked over his shoulder towards the distant woods with a look of malevolence that was clear enough in the moonlight.

Levy recognized the officer just mentioned as a major of artillery, Kincaid was his name. That look could only mean one thing.

"We'd better duck now. I think this whole area is in for some hot artillery work."

"How do you..." the words had barely left Hans' mouth when the shells and mortars started to scream and crash all around.

Levy reached for his Siddur and began to recite psalms.

Hans, fully cowed now, shuffled over to Levy's side of the trench as the ground shook from impact after impact.

"Say them with me!" Levy screamed over the noise, pointing to the Siddur he was clutching.

Levy then proceeded to shout a verse with Hans repeating after him. At first, Hans found it difficult to pronounce the Hebrew, but soon got the hang of it.

A shell would land with a thud close by, explode and then rain down dirt and material on their heads. Shaking off the debris, they would continue reciting, sometimes blowing the dirt from their mouths, and other times dusting off the prayer book.
They crouched in their hole for hours, saying chapter after chapter as the world exploded around them.

Chapter Fifteen

War can sometimes be deceiving. A quiet morning with bright sunlight; the bright, almost cloudless sky like a blue-white piece of fine china set in a dome overhead. Maybe a hint of pink reflecting on the light feathers of clouds which hung suspended above. A cool breeze blowing softly over the waving grass. A fine day indeed.

But then, the sounds of the wounded and dying soldiers are brought to the ears from all around. The smell of gunpowder and burnt trees and other things much worse as well. A pop of someone discharging their rifle at an antagonist. All of this brings the soldier back to his reality. War: the most destructive force humanity has ever brought upon itself.

Such was the case for Hans and Levy. The sun had just risen and it was indeed a glorious day, had it not been for the fact that they were wedged in a crater eight feet across and perhaps six feet wide, in between the lines at Chancellorsville, one of the bloodiest battles of the Civil War. The ghastly sounds of a battlefield the morning after had been borne on the breeze, and they shuddered to think what was waiting for them over the brim of their little underground enclave.

Peeking over the edge, they were surprised to find that they were in the middle of a moonscape. The holes created by huge shells were everywhere. Dirt piled high in some areas and scorched in others. The acrid smell of sulfur and gun-smoke was strong. The trees in what had been the copse of trees last night, were knocked down like so many toothpicks. Some torn from their roots by the sheer force of the bombardment, others splintered into fine twigs which were flung everywhere.

It was a miracle really: the fact that they had survived intact with barely a scratch.

Hans and Levy looked at each other in undisguised wonderment. 'How had they made it through the fierce bombardment without so much as a scratch?' was the unspoken thought they shared.

Hans instinctively gulped and said in a shaky voice, "I... I think we were just... It must have been that praying. God Himself protected us!"

"Indeed, it would seem as such," Levy replied in an equally tremulous tone. "Hashem seems to have stepped in. *Magen Avraham* - Abraham's shield!"

The realization that they had been saved by an open miracle was perhaps the most profound moment of their young lives. Without either knowing it at the time, through their actions that night in the trench, they had changed the course of their own history as well as that of generations to come.

The bond that formed by sharing mutual dangers and emerging intact could not be understated or broken by something as simple as serving on two sides of a conflict tearing apart a nation of brothers.

More importantly, that Jewish spark which had traveled nearly two thousand years to be present at Chancellorsville was fanned into a mighty flame in the heart of one where it had smoldered almost to extinction. In the other, that spark, which already bloomed mightily, was girded round, immune to any wind which might try to extinguish it. A Jewish soul never loses that light.

That Sunday in 1863 saw some of the most brutal fighting during the Civil War. Robert E. Lee resumed his assault against a demoralized Northern army and forced that army back on its defenses until such a point that Hooker called a retreat, pulling back across the Rappahannock. Yet another Union offensive had been shattered by the audacity of Lee and his lieutenant, Jackson. It was that great turning moment that changed the fortunes of the day, and it is still studied in army war colleges to this day.

Unfortunately for the Southern cause, they had lost one of their most important military figures. Stonewall Jackson, who had lead a corps of the Army of Northern Virginia so successfully had been grievously wounded that second night of the battle, losing his left arm.

No longer would 'Old Blue Light' terrorize the Northern commanders, leaving them unexpectedly defenseless when he would appear on their flank or rear with a force that fought with unbridled fury. Never again would General Lee try one of those sweeping maneuvers that gained so much fame for his army. Upon hearing of Jackson losing his arm, Lee was heard to remark, "He may have lost his left arm, but I have lost my right." No truer sentiment could have been stated.

Ten Days later, Jackson left this world. Pneumonia had set it in after initial improvement in his condition.

"Now, let us cross over the river," were his final words.

On that fateful battlefield that day, the two fast friends' trials and tribulations were far from over. The problem now was getting away from the fighting in a whole condition, but that was easier said than done with armies maneuvering all around them. Both of them were covered in dust, mud, and grime, so their uniforms had become unrecognizable. They might be mistaken for the enemy by either side, and be added to the casualty lists of their respective armies.

First things first, as it always is. They had to escape their hiding spot, which was a hole in the field between two very aggressive forces.

"What do you propose we do now?" Levy queried.

"I'm thinking. Quiet, please."

"It seems we're in a bind."

"I said quiet!"

"OK. I'll be quiet." Then after a few seconds: "Have a plan yet?"

"Arrrgh! Leave me to my thoughts. I almost had something and you are causing me to forget what I was thinking about! Not another word!"

"OK."

"Oy!" The frustration on his face soon wavered as he exclaimed, "I've got it! Follow my lead!"

Hans poked his head above the rim and scanned the horizon all around. Nothing stirred, not even the breeze. He squatted down again, picked up a stick from the muddy bottom of their refuge, and raised his hat a few feet above the edge. No sooner had he stretched out his arm, than a bullet whizzed through the air, leaving a clean hole through the woolen cap.

"Well, that won't work." Hans stated with more than a touch of exasperation in his voice.

"No it won't, but I'm not worried. Hashem will help us like he did the last time." Levy intoned.

"I think we'll definitely need his help *this* time, that's for sure!" Hans slumped down in the ditch and covered his face. After surviving the entire night, he was not happy about being a target this morning.

The words had hardly left his mouth when an errant cannonball suddenly blew up on the southern side. The resulting explosion and smoke, which roiled across the battlefield, was just the cover the two heroes needed to escape.

Hans pulled himself over the edge and extended a hand to Levy, who followed shortly behind. Keeping low to the ground, the dust-covered figures made off in an easterly direction, hoping for the best.

Upon reaching the nearest clump of trees, they paused.

"Well, I think we've reached the end of our adventure together." Hans stated with a touch of disappointment in his voice.

Levy caught the meaning from Hans and responded with sincerity, "Yes, this war will never be quite the same, that's for sure."

Suddenly, Hans tackled Levy, throwing him to the ground.

Levy screamed as he spat the dirt from his mouth. "What are you doing? I thought we were friends!"

Before Hans could answer, his actions became clear, and the cannonball screamed through the air, whizzing over Levy's head and splintering a nearby tree.

Levy smiled sheepishly. "I'll never learn..."

Hans smiled back and prepared to leave. "Please take care of yourself, as I would be delighted to see you when the states are reunited!"

"I will see if I can obtain permission to visit the Yankee capital when this is all over. Of course, it may be some years before they let Confederate citizens in."

The sarcasm was not lost on Hans, yet he replied, "Moreover, we are both Jewish, and I have learned if nothing else, that it supersedes all of this," while gesturing broadly. "No matter which side we may fight for individually, we are still brothers."

"Indeed it does. Well, my friend..."

They clasped hands and turned their backs on each other, each headed to more adventure and accompanying risks.

Levy turned suddenly and called out, "Hans! I've got something for you! You can return it after the war, no matter what the outcome."

With that, he thrust the precious Siddur into Hans' hands, who for his part, was speechless, and this was probably the first time in his life such a thing had happened to him.

Levy strode off into the smoke and gloom of the battlefield with a smile on his face.

When he had gathered his composure, Hans looked down at this, the sweetest of gifts that had been given to him. He flipped open the cover to find the inscription:

5-3-1863 Inst.

To my dear friend Hans,
May this siddur serve you through all the trials, tribulations, and the good times as well,
which you will face in the future. May Hashem bless you and keep you in all you do.

Truly, Your friend Levy

Chapter Sixteen

"And so," continued Aaron, "Hans would go on to participate in many more grim battles that comprised the remainder of that bloody conflict: the American Civil War. He was cited for bravery and valor during Chancellorsville, and that would eventually earn him the highest honor the United States can bestow upon its soldiers: the Medal of Honor. After the war he would never quite get over his thirst for adventure, although he would eventually marry and settle down. He actually joined a famous detective agency as a man in the field. This agency, Pinkerton's, would play a major role in the breaking up of many corrupt local governments and crime families. Hans himself was instrumental in bringing down one of the more nefarious groups in the Pennsylvania coal district called the Molly Mcguires. He never forgot his encounter with Levy, and learned enough about his religion to qualify him as a "Gabi," or assistant Rabbi, at his local congregation. He got married some years after the war and raised a small family with a deep sense of Jewish identity. One of his sons was my great grandfather. My family has been observant I guess, since right after the Civil War.

Avi was impressed. "What about Levy?" he asked.

"Well, from what I've heard, Levy would go on to fight in several more battles before finally making the ultimate sacrifice in the trenches of Petersburg a year and half after the battle at Chancellorsville. Before that, he had just enough time to marry his childhood sweetheart in a traditional Jewish ceremony and father a child. This child was born to a lonely mother only a few days after his father left this world. Being a single mother in Richmond as the Confederacy was collapsing was not the easiest of circumstances, as I'm sure you can imagine. As soon as it was practicable, mother and child were bundled off to stay with relatives in Savannah, Georgia.

This child grew up to be a leader of his community and raised a large family dedicated to Jewish ideals. One of his sons became involved with socialism and an even more radical movement called Zionism." Aaron chuckled at this and then continued. "And at the age of 50, was one of the first "Chalutzim," or pioneers, to establish a presence in the ancient Jewish holy land of Israel. After that, my family lost touch with Levy's family. Guess that's what happens over a long period of time."

Avi leaned back in his seat and was silent for some time. His thoughts were traveling back, along his own family tree.

Just then, the captain came on the intercom to let everyone know that the plane was nearing its final destination and that everyone should move the seat backs to the upright position, fasten their belts, and prepare for the landing.

Aaron and Avi had been engrossed in the story and had barely noticed the nine hours or so that the flight had taken.

Aaron looked out the window like a kid staring through the glass storefront, into a candy store. He had had an overwhelming feeling of being in a place where he belonged, as the beach slid past on the plane's final approach. In fact, as he saw the palm trees of the Tel Aviv coast swaying in the breeze, he said to himself, *"I'm home!"* without really knowing why. It must have been some ancient inborn instinct, or a spark, deep within his soul. Either way, he was surprised by his own thoughts.

Avi craned his neck to look over Aaron's shoulder. It was clear he was having the same feelings, even though this was not the first, third, or even twentieth time Avi had been in an aircraft skimming the highways that crisscrossed the Holy Land at this point; not new, but always emotional.

Suddenly and without warning, the plane jerked upward and the people onboard gasped at the sudden change of direction. A few passengers screamed, and children clutched their parents' arms.

Aaron gripped the armrests and his knuckles turned white with the pressure. *What was going on?!*

The pilot was on the speaker almost immediately, first in Hebrew, and then in English. "Uh folks, we have a small problem near the airport. Nothing to be alarmed about, but we may need to circle around a bit until the problem is cleared up."

Avi, no stranger to intense situations as a former Sayeret Matkal, didn't lose his cool. Instead, he did what he was trained to do. He removed himself from the situation and thought objectively. What "problem" at or near the airport would make the pilot pull such a maneuver, especially in the crowded airspace around Ben Gurion International Airport? Maybe the news had picked it up already.

He reached into his pocket and pulled out his phone. Typing in his password, he quickly switched off the airplane mode. The bars on his phone lit up right away, indicating a connection.

The news on Channel 2 was the first thing that came up on Google when he searched for the airport they were supposed to be landing at in the next few minutes. His hand shot to his mouth, as he let out a gasp, despite his self-control. A Hamas-linked terrorist cell had broken through the tight ring of security that surrounded Ben Gurion International Airport and had set up a Stinger missile, which was currently trained on the plane they were in!

Apparently, the cement that was headed into Gaza was not exactly for "humanitarian purposes," and the terrorists in control there had used it to build a tunnel with the exit a few kilometers from Israel's largest airport.

Aaron, nervous as anyone would be in the situation, glanced over Avi's shoulder and nearly fainted at the news.

Avi looked around at the other passengers, some of whom had recently received the news via text from loved ones or by watching the news on their own phones.

Needless to say, panic ensued with screaming, yelling, and all of the expected reactions being displayed. A shaking stewardess attempted, with little success, to calm the travelers down. Another flight attendant was cowering in the corner and mumbling to herself; not much help to anyone, including herself.

"Hashem Yerachaim! Please help us!" Avi shouted.

Aaron heard this and reached for the Siddur again. "Here Avi, say this with me!!" and with that, began to recite the 23rd Psalm.

Avi joined his traveling companion in earnest praying with all of his might, to a higher power. This was something he never, had he had the time to think, would have done. It seemed so natural when there was no one else but God above to address his appeal.

The lead terrorist held the radio to his ear and mumbled a few words in Arabic to headquarters. He then gave a sign with his hand to the bearded young man with the stinger anti-aircraft missile who raised the rocket and clicked off the safety.

Aiming carefully like he had practiced many times before, Ahmad Mashal exhaled deeply and held his breath. This was not an easy shot, even with the guidance system that was built into the projectile. He had to release it exactly at the proper time in order to take down the jet. He and the rest of his cohorts prayed in unison that they would succeed.

They all knew with certainty that this was a mission they would never return from, but if they could just take down one plane, Israel would never be the same. Major airlines would refuse to land there and Israel would be effectively cut off from the rest of the world. A powerful bargaining chip would be placed in the Hamas arsenal alongside the indiscriminate rocket fire and bus bombings. Israel would be forced to give up large swaths of territory in order to "guarantee" peace. From there, it would be only a matter of time until Israel and all of its people would be forced into the sea! A goal for which the ultimate sacrifice was well worth making.

While the 747 circled the runway, all the while in the sights of the terrorist missile, help from God was on its way in the form of the Israeli Defense Force and its high tech helicopters, drones, and satellite reconnaissance. In a bunker in an undisclosed location, somewhere within Israel a screen flashed the gray images that are so familiar to those who have watched the news and heard a general describe the latest successful elimination of an arch terrorist.

The controller adjusted his headset and watched for the perfect moment. There it was! The grainy figures of the Jihadist team became clearer as the targeting computers resolved the strike coordinates. He cleared his channel with the flick of a button and spoke the terse orders:

"This is Eagle 1 to Sparrow 2. Come in."

"Copy that, Eagle 1. This is Sparrow 2. "

"We have target acquisition. Fire at your convenience."

The pilot of the "Tzefa" helicopter knew that meant to fire now. The small, light helicopter, which was a beefed up version of the Bell AH-1 Cobra attack helicopter, rotated so as to release its deadly fire in the appropriate direction. The missiles shot out from under the pylons and streaked across the landscape.

Ahmad, the jihadist, prepared to release the missile on the defenseless passengers when he heard a slight whooshing sound. Half a second later, he and his entire team were vaporized by the hellfire missile's direct strike, aided by the Stinger rocket's charge. When the dust and smoke dissipated, there was nothing left but some drops of blood, a few strips of burnt cloth, and a small crater where the tunnel exit had been.

Aboard the airplane, a few tense moments passed as the news reported the most minute details about what was happening. Some were true and some were rumors, but one thing was clear: the passengers were in grave danger, and so was the entire Israeli nation. Suddenly, as Aaron and Avi looked out the window, smoke erupted from the spot the terrorist had been aiming from. They thought it was the smoke from the hand held rocket and prayed even harder, thinking this may be the last thing that they ever did. When nothing happened, they opened their eyes and dared to look out the window. What they saw was barren earth. No terrorist group, no missile, no danger.

Chapter Seventeen

Aaron and Avi stood together at the baggage claim, chatting and exchanging contact info. After a safe landing and a ninety minute wait on the tarmac for the Army to secure the airport, the passengers were free to go. Avi's credentials with the Israeli military had allowed them to pass through security and customs in a matter of minutes.

"So, Avi, where did you say your family was from again?"

"Originally? The American south somewhere. I think I might have had some family who fought in the civil war too, but never really researched it. That's what my mother told me, at least."

Suddenly, they both stopped dead in their tracks. It struck both of them like a lightning bolt simultaneously.

Slapping his forehead, Aaron was the first to speak. "What an absolute miracle!"

"Aaron, are you thinking what I'm thinking?" Avi blurted.

"It's incredible!"

"How is it possible?"

"Simple! The Shield of Abraham! There's my bag! But first, I've got something for you! I'm really just returning it to its original owner!" With that, Aaron thrust the Siddur into Avi's hand, grabbed his bag, and left, leaving a stunned Avi Levy with his mouth agape and a whirl of emotions to deal with.

General Thomas J. Jackson

General Robert E. Lee

General Joseph Hooker

General Daniel E. Sickles

General Darius N. Couch

General O.O. Howard

General Jeb Stuart

Dowdall's Tavern - Howards Headquarters during the battle until driven from it by Jackson's assault on May 2, 1863.

Chancellorsville House - Hooker's headquarters for most of the battle

Lithograph of the death of General Jackson. Notice that it is depicted as happening during the day. The event actually occurred after sunset, however.

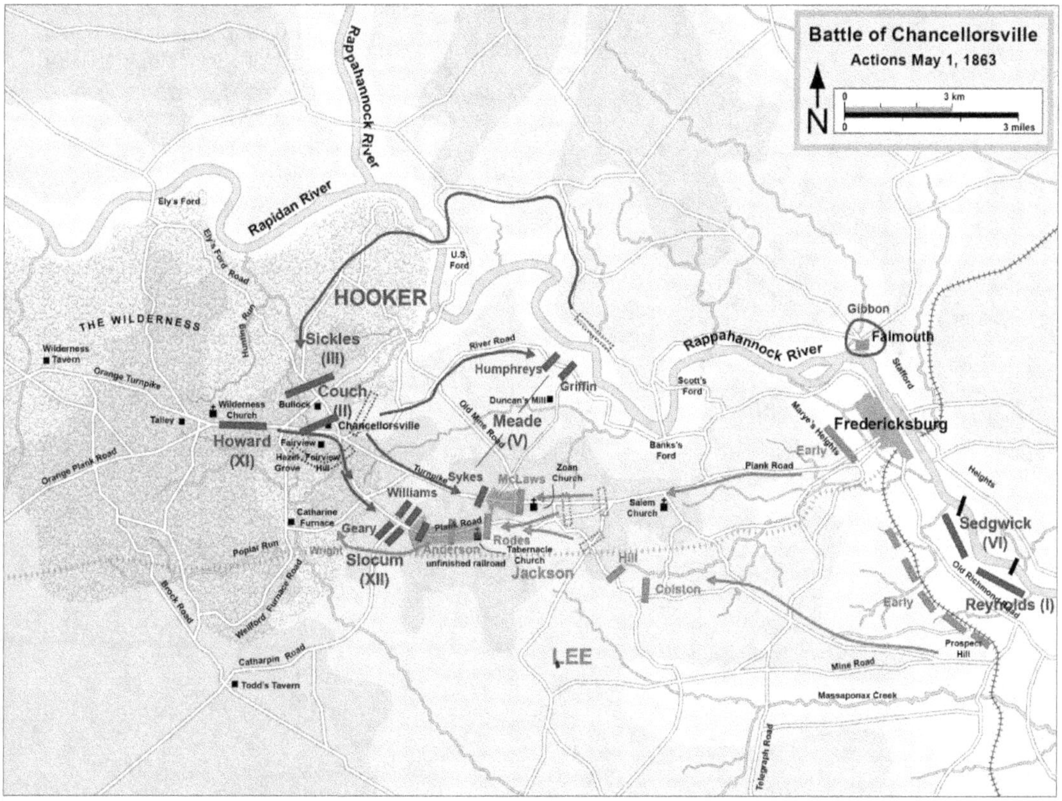
Battle of Chancellorsville
Actions May 1, 1863
N
3 km
3 miles
Rappahannock River
Rapidan River
Ely's Ford
Ely's Ford Road
U.S. Ford
HOOKER
THE WILDERNESS
Wilderness Tavern
Orange Turnpike
Hunting Run
Sickles (III)
Couch (II)
Bullock
Wilderness Church
Talley
Chancellorsville
Howard (XI)
Fairview
Hazel Grove
Fairview Hill
Orange Plank Road
Catharine Furnace
Poplar Run
Brock Road
Welford Furnace Road
Catharpin Road
Todd's Tavern
Williams
Geary
Wright
Slocum (XII)
Anderson
unfinished railroad
Plank Road
Turnpike
Sykes
McLaws
Zoan Church
Rodes
Tabernacle Church
Jackson
Hill
Colston
LEE
River Road
Humphreys
Griffin
Duncan's Mill
Old Mine Road
Meade (V)
Scott's Ford
Banks's Ford
Salem Church
Plank Road
Gibbon
Falmouth
Stafford
Marye's Heights
Early
Fredericksburg
Heights
Sedgwick (VI)
Old Richmond Road
Early
Reynolds (I)
Prospect Hill
Mine Road
Massaponax Creek
Telegraph Road

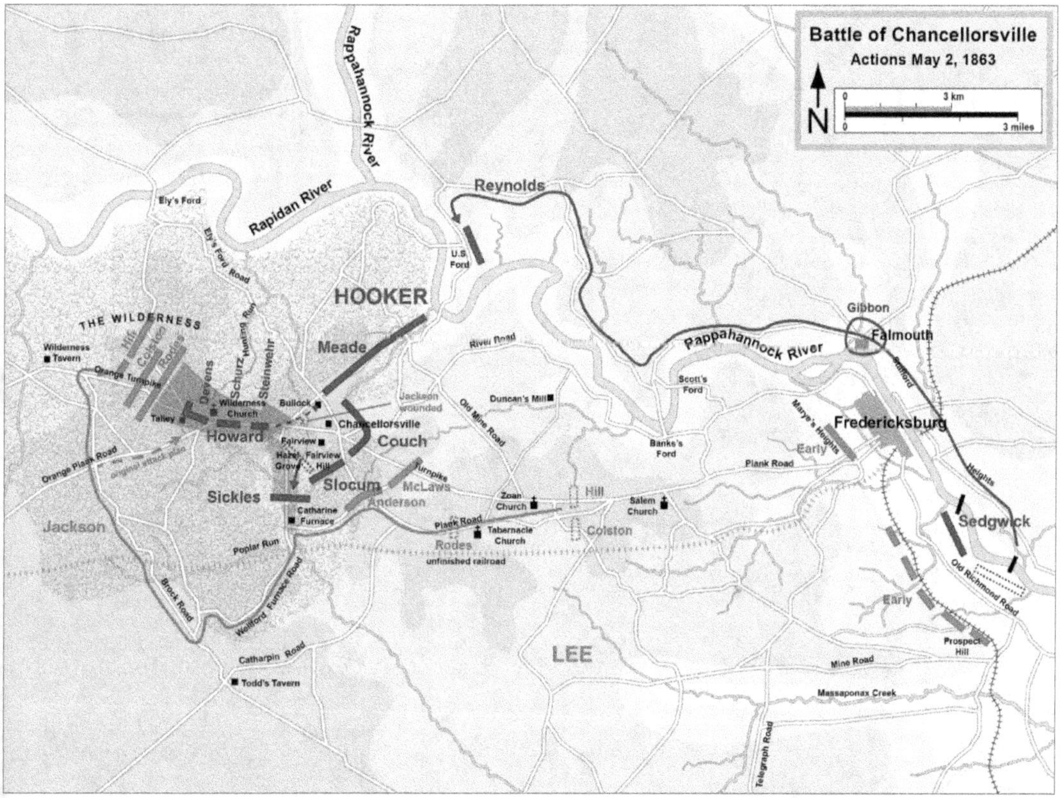
Battle of Chancellorsville
Actions May 2, 1863
N
3 km
3 miles
Rappahannock River
Rapidan River
Ely's Ford
Ely's Ford Road
Reynolds
U.S. Ford
HOOKER
THE WILDERNESS
Wilderness Tavern
Orange Turnpike
Hill
Colston
Rodes
Devens
Schurz
Steinwehr
Hunting Run
Meade
Bullock
Wilderness Church
Talley
Jackson wounded
Chancellorsville
Howard
Couch
Fairview
Hazel Grove
Fairview Hill
Orange Plank Road
original attack plan
Slocum
Sickles
Catharine Furnace
McLaws
Anderson
Turnpike
Jackson
Poplar Run
Brock Road
Welford Furnace Road
Catharpin Road
Todd's Tavern
Zoan Church
Plank Road
Tabernacle Church
Rodes
unfinished railroad
Hill
Colston
LEE
River Road
Duncan's Mill
Old Mine Road
Scott's Ford
Banks's Ford
Salem Church
Plank Road
Gibbon
Falmouth
Stafford
Marye's Heights
Early
Fredericksburg
Heights
Sedgwick
Old Richmond Road
Early
Prospect Hill
Mine Road
Massaponax Creek
Telegraph Road

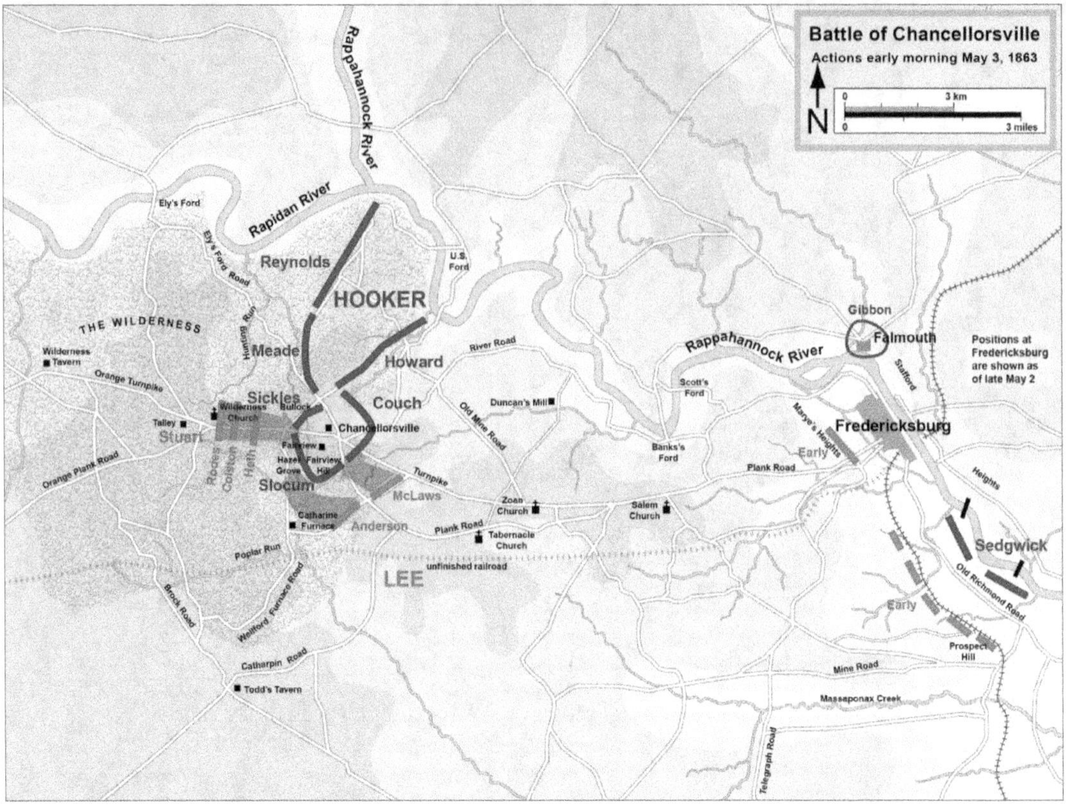

Battle of Chancellorsville
Actions early morning May 3, 1863
N
3 km
3 miles
Rappahannock River
Rapidan River
Ely's Ford
Ely's Ford Road
U.S. Ford
Reynolds
HOOKER
THE WILDERNESS
Hunting Run
Meade
Howard
Wilderness Tavern
Orange Turnpike
River Road
Sickles
Couch
Duncan's Mill
Talley
Wilderness Church
Bullock
Chancellorsville
Stuart
Fairview
Rodes
Colston
Heth
Hazel Grove
Fairview Hill
Old Mine Road
Orange Plank Road
Slocum
Turnpike
McLaws
Catharine Furnace
Anderson
Zoan Church
Plank Road
Tabernacle Church
Salem Church
Poplar Run
unfinished railroad
LEE
Brock Road
Wellford Furnace Road
Catharpin Road
Todd's Tavern
Gibbon
Falmouth
Positions at Fredericksburg are shown as of late May 2
Scott's Ford
Stafford
Marye's Heights
Fredericksburg
Banks's Ford
Early
Plank Road
Heights
Sedgwick
Old Richmond Road
Early
Prospect Hill
Mine Road
Massaponax Creek
Telegraph Road

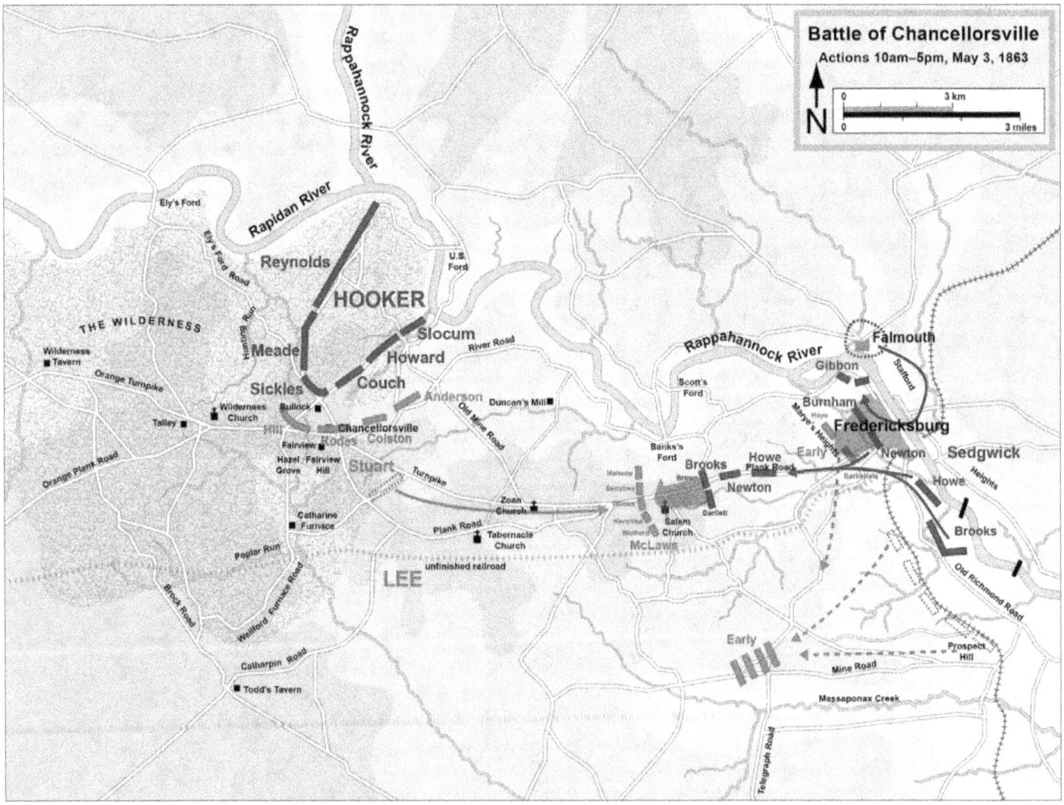

Battle of Chancellorsville
Actions 10am–5pm, May 3, 1863
N
3 km
3 miles
Rappahannock River
Rapidan River
Ely's Ford
Ely's Ford Road
U.S. Ford
Reynolds
HOOKER
THE WILDERNESS
Hunting Run
Meade
Slocum
Howard
River Road
Wilderness Tavern
Orange Turnpike
Couch
Sickles
Anderson
Duncan's Mill
Talley
Wilderness Church
Bullock
Chancellorsville
Hill
Rodes
Colston
Old Mine Road
Fairview
Hazel Grove
Fairview Hill
Stuart
Turnpike
Orange Plank Road
Zoan Church
Catharine Furnace
Plank Road
Tabernacle Church
Poplar Run
unfinished railroad
LEE
Brock Road
Wellford Furnace Road
Catharpin Road
Todd's Tavern
Falmouth
Gibbon
Stafford
Scott's Ford
Burnham
Marye's Heights
Fredericksburg
Banks's Ford
Brooks
Howe
Plank Road
Early
Newton
Sedgwick
Newton
Howe
Heights
Salem Church
McLaws
Brooks
Old Richmond Road
Early
Prospect Hill
Mine Road
Massaponax Creek
Telegraph Road

JONAH REVISTED

April 16th 1861

The rooster crowed, and Levy Isaac opened his eyes wearily. Looking out his window on the second floor of the large mansion which took up a sizable portion of land on the immense plantation his family owned, he could see the slaves already making their way towards the distant fields. As the sun rose over the trees, it colored the sky delicate shades of pink and blue. A thin pall of mist hung like a loose sheet over the fields, and a cool breeze blew in through the window, making the curtains rustle. This was Levy's favorite time of day, but even if it hadn't been, he still would have jumped from his bed with anticipation knowing what day it was. For today was the day when his uncle Moses would visit!

It was spring 1861, near Chestnut Grove, VA, which is close to the big city of Richmond, VA. South Carolina had seceded from the Union more than four months ago and the Federal garrison at Fort Sumter had been fired upon by the Southern hero, P.T. Beauregard. The Federal response had been swift, and the declaration of war against the seceding states had dragged the entire nation into a war. Both sides hoped they would be successful and the war would not continue that long. Little did they know that 4 years later the southern half of the country would be laid to waste and over half a million of its sons would be buried.

That mattered little to Levy now, as he dressed quickly and ran downstairs to breakfast. His father, tall and broad shouldered, was seated at the head of the table. He was in the midst of making the blessing after his morning meal. A busy day awaited him overseeing his large holdings.

"Levy, how are you feeling this morning?" he asked when he finished his supplications.

"Fine, Father. Did um... did Uncle Moses come yet?"

"Not yet," Levy's father answered with a smile. "He should be along shortly though. I know you love his little inventions."

Levy couldn't deny it. His uncle's imaginative solutions to everyday problems always fascinated him.

"Sure do Father! I can't wait to see what he's working on now! Why did you say he's coming again?"

The truth was that Uncle Moses was coming for a little working capital. Levy's father, being the more successful brother, financially and otherwise, felt responsible for keeping his younger sibling out of trouble which meant keeping him busy with his "inventions" which incidentally never worked exactly as planned.

"He said he had to try out a new device for making the chickens produce larger eggs. Do you remember that time he tried to make a machine for milking the cows? He nearly lost all fingers on his hand not to mention scaring the daylights out of the heifers!" He laughed.

"Yes I do Father! And the slaves said that God Himself was coming down from the mountain with all that noise!" Levy doubled over with laughter.

When he caught his breath again he exclaimed between gasps "Or that device for turning manure into bricks! He...he.... he created an explosion they could see from the river! "

Levy's father could barely speak from mirth but managed to get out "Your... Your mother couldn't... Ha! I don't know if she ever got the smell out of the curtains! Oh! Ha! Dear Lord that was funny!" and he broke down into a fit of laughter along with his son.

When they both regained their composure, a rather serious looking woman, Levy's mother, looked in on them. "What is it you two are laughing about?"

Mr. Isaac was the first to regain his composure. "We were just talking about Uncle Moses' inventions!

"Oh, don't remind me! If I never see him again, it will be too soon!"

"Mother," Levy's father said with some hesitation "I feel you won't be too happy about this then. He'll be here shortly or I'm mistaken. I thought I told you about it."

"Ribono Shel Olam![5] He'll wreck this place yet with his crazy inventions! Why is he coming?"

"Just to visit I suppose." Mr. Isaac mumbled sheepishly.

"I very much doubt that! He's here for more money to fund more crackpot projects! We'll discuss this later. Levy doesn't need to hear this," she announced while looking at Mr. Isaac with more than just a mere touch of frustration.

Just then, a very frazzled servant ran in with his wife huddling behind him, glancing nervously towards the front of the house.

"Master!" he announced pointing out the window "I do believe the apocalypse is upon us! There's a right scary monster over thar, breathing fire!"

The smell of smoke was accompanied by a hideous rumble, punctuated with crackling explosions.

Running to the bay window, the family arrived in time to witness a man in a leather cap, sitting on the seat of what looked like a large wheeled, wooden wagon, with some sort of oven perched atop. The contraption seemed to be moving under its own power, jolting and swaying from side to side, spitting fire and smoke all the while. Servants were running in all directions in an attempt to avoid being bowled over. Suddenly, it shot forward across the wide, front lawn and careened into the garden, landing on its side.

---

[5] Translation: "Master of the World" A common term in Judaism sometimes used as an expression of exasperation.

Emerging from the dust cloud and brushing himself off, Uncle Moses coughed a few times and produced a rather dumb grin spreading from ear to ear.

"Solomon! Did you see that!" he shouted to Levy's father, who had emerged from the front door of the house.

He strode across the broad lawn with outstretched arms towards his older brother. "It works! It works! My auto-wagon works!"

"Indeed!" the lady of the house exclaimed while exiting. "You've scared the servants half to death and the cows' milk has probably turned sour in their udders! You just don't know how to make a quiet entrance, do you?"

"What is she so angry about?" Moses looked at his brother with an incredulous expression. "It works! Isn't that what matters?!"

Throwing up her hands, Mrs. Isaac turned and stomped into the house.

As they were all sitting around the table eating lunch later that day, Levy's father brought up the topic of the unrest raging throughout the country.

Levy's father was in doubt as to the advisability of going to war. "Mark my words, this war will lead to tremendous bloodshed and destruction. No chance exists that the United States will allow nearly half its land and a third of its population to establish its own country without putting up a tremendous fight."

Asher, Levy's brother, had come in from the fields to join the family for lunch. He was seated next to his father towards the head of the long, oaken table.

"I believe in a state's right to govern itself!" he was fervently declaring while pounding his fist on the table. "I will defend our home, Virginia, if attacked by the Yankees!"

His father looked uncomfortable and glanced at his wife, who was seated at the far end opposite him.

Clearing his throat, Mr. Isaac said, "I'm not excited about the prospect of seeing you in any war Asher, but I agree that if attacked, we must defend ourselves and... "

Levy barged in on the conversation. "Father, I've spoken at some length with Rabbi Cohen at the Synagogue. He was very much against any sort of war. He says it's the bane of humanity! He's also against slavery, even if most people still practice it. He cited a section of the Talmud[6] that states, 'One who acquires a slave, acquires a master!' We can't treat our slaves like chattel!"

Asher was quick to respond, "Who says this is about slaves? This is about our rights as free people living in a free country; to govern ourselves!"

"Your brother is correct, Levy," his father responded. "This struggle is about states' rights more than slavery. The North is looking to destroy our way of life."

"But isn't our way of life all about slavery?" Levy blurted.

"Yes, but..."

---

[6] Kedushin 22a

Levy's mother stepped in to halt the conversation before it became heated. "Levy, please respect your father! And Asher, don't yell at your brother!"

Everyone listened to mother and was silent.

Uncle Moses, who had been staring at the soup tureen, no doubt thinking of some new invention that would change the world, blurted out, "I... I shall lead one of my ideas into history and make my name famous in the process!"

All turned toward the speaker, some with rolling eyes, and others with expressions of wonderment and bemusement plastered across this faces.

Moses looked around equally surprised. He then stood and saluted the company before going back to attacking his food.

March 9th, 1862

A middle-aged man peered out over Virginia's largest natural harbor, Hampton Roads, the deep body of water at the confluence of the James River and Chesapeake Bay. He looked on with something akin to interest mixed with wonderment, as the gigantic form of the CSS Merrimack, the ironclad battleship, made its sluggish way towards the stranded Federal warship, the USS Minnesota. Removing his glasses, the man cleaned them with the rag he always carries with him, replaced them back on the bridge of his nose, and squinted through the smoke and mist, as did so many others that fateful day in order to see the drama play out over the deep water. In happier times, it had been a major shipping channel instead of the focal point of the Naval war happening in the Eastern part of the country.

The sailors on the Northern ship made ready the cannons, gunpowder, and cannonballs with which they would attempt to ward off, if not destroy the approaching monster. They spread sand on the wooden decks of their ship to avoid any added possibilities of slipping on the blood that was sure to be spilled during the impending confrontation. The surgeons got their tools of their respective trades out of their velvet cases and made sure they were sharp. The "tools" were mainly implements for sawing off unlucky sailors' shattered limbs.

Yet, there was confidence on the Minnesota, for just off the starboard side was the USS Monitor. Described by no less a personage than Abraham Lincoln as a "cheese box on a raft," this sausage-shaped vessel sat very low in the water, with its cylindrical turret rising from the center. Contained within the turret were two of the most powerful guns available for seafaring vessels at that time. The 11-inch rifled Dahlgrens could punch a hole in the side of a fortress or ship like it was going through paper. The turret itself was an innovation that allowed the ship to operate in shallow water and fire in any direction without having to turn the entire vessel to face its enemy.

This feature, combined with the shallow draft, which is the ability to travel in shallow waters, was the perfect foil to the Confederate ship, which was a floating mountain of iron, studded with cannons. It had been renamed the Virginia after having originally been called the Merrimack. The South had managed to resurrect it from its watery grave in the Elizabeth River and fit it with iron plating strong enough to withstand massive cannon fire. It was heavily armed for offensive operations with ten guns and a battering ram for close quarters combat.

The day before, the Virginia had managed to wreak havoc on the blockading Northern fleet, sinking two huge ships of the line[7] and grounding three others. Now, it was under the command of the executive officer, Lieutenant Jones, after its original captain Buchanan had been injured in the fighting on the prior day.

At first, no one aboard the Virginia noticed the vessel lying next to its intended target until it was within a few hundred yards. Now, the Monitor "swam" out to confront its antagonist, and the battle began in earnest.

Shots and shells ricocheted off the iron sheets of both ships while the actual concussions shook the very souls of those within. Ear drums burst and sailors fell screaming from their posts as the shock waves pounded through the metal interiors of both boats. The battle raged on; it was the first encounter of its kind, where two iron-clad ships fought each other without either side gaining an advantage. The Confederate ship was the possessor of the ability to throw more metal at its opponent, while the Monitor had superior maneuverability and the capability of retreating to shallower water if things became too "hot."

The Monitor eventually retired from the battle to switch command after its own commander became disabled. The Virginia had hit the pilot house with a vicious shot that knocked Lieutenant Worden out of action. Upon returning to its station of protecting the Minnesota, it discovered that due to some miscommunication, the Virginia had herself retired, and thus the battle had ended with the Monitor in possession of the "field."

Both sides claimed victory, but one thing was abundantly clear to a certain observer: the South would never beat the marine blockade (which was squeezing the life out of the Confederacy) on the water's surface, no matter what the Southern Navy brought to bear. The Northern Army just had too many resources.

"The blockade must be defeated under the surface! A SUB-marine vessel is what is needed!" the man exclaimed while pounding one fist into the other. "I will build it *and* pilot it to victory!" And with that, Moses Isaac turned and hurried off to his own "works" so he could create this revolutionary vessel.

---

[7] Main battle ships of the time

Later that day

"Bill, get up! We've work to do!" Moses yelled at his apprentice as he burst through the doors of his "workshop," which was the name by which he fondly referred to the musty, dusty storage room which doubled as his laboratory for special inventions. It was located above the main offices of the Tredegar Ironworks.

The Tredegar iron foundry was the South's largest, and it was the source of the majority of cannons and other artillery used in the present war. Its location in fact, had been one of the major reasons that the Confederate capital had been moved to Richmond, Virginia from Montgomery, Alabama.[8] This was done in order for the war department to be closer to the production of the various implements necessary to prosecute the fight against the Yankee "oppressors".

In any case, Moses, through the influence of his well-connected older brother Solomon, had been given a minor position in the war department, inventing new ways to visit destruction on the opposing armies. Thus far, he had managed to visit destruction on his own laboratory twice, a wagon, and some poor horse's mane. The nag had been loaned to him by someone who he had met in a local tavern and turned out to be a colonel named Ashby in Jackson's army, which was now fighting in the Shenandoah Valley. That was probably the last time he would try an experiment on a live subject. All in all, he had not been that successful.

That was why Moses was so excited right now. He finally had a chance to do something for the war effort and be the hero he always wanted to be.

"Bill, put the lamp near the table and bring me my quill and ink!"

Within the hour, the thing started to take shape on the cream colored paper on the desk. The various tubes, pipes, and tanks were sketched into a long, steam-pipe shaped iron form.

In Moses' mind the submarine seemed to jump from the page, but would it work? There was only one way to find out, and that *was to build it.*

May 9th 1862

Moses blew the residue off the rivet that held part of the hull together and sat down exhausted. Mopping his brow with a gloved hand, he was able to survey with pride, his handiwork. They had been working day and night for the past few months on the submersible and it was taking shape nicely.

The old building down by the docks was covered in a thin layer of dust with creaking boards, a musty smell, and all the other things that go along with a building that has been

---

[8] Ruins of Tredegar Ironworks, Richmond, Va. April, 1865
Brady National Photographic Art Gallery (Washington, D.C.) (1858 - ?)

neglected for some years. From the outside, it appeared to be a decaying shack; slightly greenish from moss growth around the hazy windows. Within it, half submerged in water; lay the coppery creation that was Moses' masterpiece.

It had been a hard go, to say the least. The Confederate war department wasn't exactly well-funded, and spent most of its meager budget on casting cannons and making rifles. There was precious little left for "special projects" like the one Moses had thought of. In fact, there was almost no assistance forthcoming aside from tacit support in the form of leaving him to his devices and not directing him to work on some more mundane project, like fuses for shells or bearings for canon wheels. No money meant that he had to procure his own materials to build his masterpiece. And that is what had him worried just now. He needed more: more copper to finish it up, and he hadn't gotten any in a few days. The work was taking its toll on them both, but stopping was not possible now that they had come this far.

Where was Bill anyway?

His loyal assistant had been the main forager and obtainer of material. The copper color of the submarine was due to the fact that most of the metal came from the abandoned stills in the area, as their brewers were out fighting the war. It also helped that the metal had the special property of not reacting with water. Instead, copper reacts with air, forming a blackish, brown coating that actually protects the underlying material. No rust meant no holes, hence the extreme suitability of the metal for a submarine. True, it was heavy, but it would float. At least its creator hoped it would.

Bill had discovered the ownerless condition of most of the stills after he went on a visit to his favorite maker, only to find the nest empty and the bird flown, so to speak. After imbibing a few drops, he tripped over the apparatus, knocking loose a good quantity of metal. Lying on the ground in his inebriated state, he realized that there was metal to be had here and then possibly elsewhere at other such stills. Grabbing a sheet of the shattered tank, he made his way back to the shack and his boss, Moses.

Bill had left to get more materials and had not returned for some days. Had something happened to him? The work could not continue without him, and yet they must finish before the chance to test out the craft was gone. If the war ended soon, as it appeared it might, what with Fort Donelson and Fort Henry falling in the West, along with 12,000 of the Confederacy's best troops, the opportunity for trying out the concept would be lost forever.

Shouting brought Moses out of his reverie and the crash of something hard outside made him spring up from his work.

"What, er... who goes there?" he exclaimed, reaching for his old musket.

With an earsplitting bang, Bill blew through the door, falling to the floor with the remnants of the door preceding and following him down. Scrambling to his feet, he had the look on his face of a hunted animal. His scared eyes bulged out of the sockets as he looked around for a place to hide, and then dove behind a chest of tools.

Moses had just gotten to his feet when a burly, elderly man strode through the door with a serious look on his craggy features.

"Where's he gone; that idiot?!"

"Wh...Who? Where has who gone?" Moses sputtered, trying to wrap his head around the situation.

"That confounded still wrecker! He's made off with most of my tank, not to mention a good jug of the best brew in the area!"

The speaker was a man closer to 60 than 50, with a wide jaw, massive shoulders, and the body of a tree trunk. His head was covered with a soft flop hat and he wore nothing under his overalls; his bare feet were sticking out from the tattered legs. A thin stubble of white facial hair covered his sunburned face. A typical mountain man if ever there was one.

"Oh, Bill?" the inventor spoke in a trembling voice.

"Have you seen him?"

"No..."

"He's behind that there chest isn't he? Come out o' there you low down filcher!"

The old man walked over to the tool container and began banging on it with the butt of his gun while screaming unintelligible utterances, causing Bill to squirm and look for an escape route.

Moses was not the bravest of men, but this was ridiculous, and it had to be stopped. He fired his gun at the ceiling, which brought a stop to the melee that was unfolding in the shack, along with a shower of dust and wood chips.

Moses shouted, "Enough! I've got it double-loaded! The next one hits your backside! This ends now!"

The old man spun on his heel, his face red with exertion. "Okay, Mr. Buck Shot! Who's going to pay for my still?"

"What's your name?" the inventor spoke with more force than he thought himself capable of.

"Tom Cairns. But those who knows me, just calls me Cairns."

"Right. Cairns, well, if you knew the noble cause for which Bill over there," pointing to his still shaken assistant, "has been 'borrowing' your still pieces."

"Tell me then, and maybe I'll let him walk out of here."

"Ahem," Moses cleared his throat. "Your copper will be used for the walls of the underwater boat that will save the Confederacy from starvation! It lies almost done, right there, and you will not be allowed to stop history!"

"Indeed that would be helpful. Okay Mr... eh, what is your name?"

"Moses Isaacs."

"Okay, Moses Isaac, what do you know about seafaring?"

The inventor had to admit, "Not much... but I know science, and I know my creation will work!"

"Maybe so, but who will test it? Who will steer it? Who will make sure it can be used for battle?"

"You have experience, Cairns?"

"Aye! When I was a lad, I was with Jackson at New Orleans![9] I manned a cannon for Lafitte when he was making the British squeal! I landed a ship o' the line at Vera Cruz when Scott was heading to Mexico City! Have I experience, he asks?!"

"Indeed. Okay, well are you volunteering then?"

"If it means saving our country, then yes! Tell me more about your craft!"

"Well then! Here are the plans on the wall here! You see how I've designed it so the depth can be controlled by these ballast devices? If you really need to rise quickly, I have an emergency iron plate here that can be unscrewed from the inside of the craft. The reduction in weight should lift the submersible to the surface within a few seconds, from up to 50 feet below the water!"

Moses went on to explain more parts of the sub with Cairns interjecting every now and again with suggestions as to how to make it more seaworthy.

Finally, as the sun set, they were done discussing the ship, and they shook hands.

"I'm in, Moses!" Cairns exclaimed. "I shall be here early tomorrow and we'll continue working on this together! You'll be the pilot and I'll train your crew when it's ready."

"Deal, sir! You've got a deal!" a beaming Moses declared.

As they were preparing to leave, Moses turned back and asked, "Where is Bill anyway?"

Bill hopped up from behind the tool chest and rubbed the sleep from his eyes, and with a sheepish grin, began cleaning up.

"Well he's got a good heart anyway..." Moses offered, looking at Cairns with an air of resignation and a shrug of his shoulders.

---

[9] One of the most one-sided victories in American history, it actually occurred in 1815 *after* the Treaty of Ghent was signed officially ending the War of 1812. The British lost a good portion of their invading force to American guns behind fortifications. The commanding British general, the hero of the Battle of Toulouse, Sir Edward Pakenham, was killed and sent home in a barrel intended for war booty obtained from the Americans. Jean Lafitte and his band of pirates took part in this battle which involved an ambush of the British camp by ship on the night of the 24th of December 1814.

July 5th, 1863

Mr. Boeteler tipped his hat at the waitress after she set his drink down in front of him. The dark corners of this particular tavern were populated by some of the shadier characters in wartime Richmond. Everyone, from smugglers to spies and all manner of charlatans and rapscallions could be found here.

Yet, here in this dimly lit ramshackle bar, was a very interesting figure who didn't seem to fit in with the rest of the crowd. Wild-haired with some sort of protective glasses perched atop his head; he was blabbering excitedly to his two companions. One was a youthful, rather dumb looking individual who looked down in his drink often, and the other was a bulky, weather-bitten, elderly looking fellow who seemed more at home in the hills than in the urban society of the capital of the Confederacy.

Boeteler was desperate. He had been given the task by the Confederate Congress of moving along special projects focused on ridding the Confederacy of the blockade, which stifled its industry and trade with the outside world. Numerous ideas had been bandied about and actual inventions had been created without any positive results. Things were getting quite serious and he was grasping at straws, looking for a way to solve the dilemma or face economic ruin, and the loss of the independence; so much blood had been spilled already. With that in mind, he seated himself with this motley crew.

The crazy inventor sitting across from him was spewing all sorts of scientific jargon and mathematical calculations, but he seemed passionate enough about his project.

"Once the Union realizes what we've got, they'll have to drop their infernal blockade!" he was saying.

"Well sir, pardon my curiosity, but what type of weapon are you referring to?"

With that, Moses proceeded to explain the submarine to this messenger of Congress.

"It's made of what?" an incredulous Boeteler asked.

As Moses was about to answer, a grey-clad soldier burst through the door. The blinding midday sunlight streamed in behind him, causing those inside to shield their eyes from the searing brightness.

"Vicksburg has fallen! Grant has taken it, and some twenty-nine thousand of our men with it!"

Along with the still fresh news of the disaster of Gettysburg, the loss of Vicksburg caused the fortunes of the Confederacy to dim significantly. Dejection is not an adequate word to describe the effect of this announcement on the clients of the tavern.

When Boeteler was able to speak again, he looked Moses square in the eye and declared fervently; "You had me interested before in your project, but this news..." he coughed into his handkerchief, "This news changes all. We must do something quickly! I will find you more funding and a crew for your submersible. It may be our last hope!"

July 26th, 1863

Mr. Boeteler burst through the door of the dockside shack. "I've got your crew, Moses!" The inventor and Cairns looked up from their work in a state of surprise.

"Well, that was mighty quick, Mr. Congressman!" Cairns spake, a hint of sarcasm in his gruff voice.

"I did the best I can, Mr. Cairns... It's only been three weeks."

Cairns merely grunted in response as Moses exuded excitement and removed his protective glasses. "Well then, let's meet them!"

"Just what I was thinking!" the politician stated emphatically.

Out in the sunlight stood the men who had volunteered for this special assignment. Among them were the usual assortment of gnarled, seafarer types. One sailor stood out from the rest, however. He was a tall, commanding young man in his late twenties, with nutcracker jaws and an air of superiority that swirled around him. His pressed uniform belied a certain arrogance, much the same as the person wearing it conveyed a similar message.

He stepped forward with a salute as Mr. Boeteler passed through the door. "Sir, all of the men are present for duty as requested!"

"Yes. Very good, Mr. Pine," and then, turning to Moses, who had followed him through the door, "This is Lieutenant Pine, and these are your men. They have all the experience you could ask for and will do their job as well as any that have sailed before them. Mr Pines, please introduce your men."

As Pines barked out their names, each sailor stepped forward.

"Phillips!"

The old tar[10] who presented himself was all skin and bones. He doffed his old cap and stood at attention for review. "Sir!"

"Effers!"

The sunburned and short man with the intent squint and muscular arms of a harpooner, which in fact he had been, stepped forward smartly, his drooping black mustache glimmering in the sunshine. "Aye!" he exclaimed.

"Grozinzky!"

---

[10] Slang for sailor

A lanky, sallow looking fellow presented himself with his lank hair and yellowy eyes, which indicated scurvy or some other malady caused by a harsh life spent at sea, fighting the elements and the rum bottle.

And so continued the review until all of the crew had been introduced.

Satisfied, Boeteler turned to the inventor, saying, "Now Moses, if you will please explain to them what your vessel is all about."

Moses proceeded to tell them about his project and what their purpose was. He also explained to them that he would be the captain of record. This provoked a few snickers from the crew. After all, the inventor was more of a well... an inventor, with his crazy hair and frail looking frame.

After he finished his speech, Boeteler asked, "Is everything clear?"

Pines preempted the crew with a sneer and a question. "Just to understand sir, we are to be the crew on this historic craft on its historic maiden voyage, and he," pointing to Moses, "will be the captain? If you don't mind my saying so, it seems this Jew (he said this word with an especially disdainful emphasis) hasn't the required experience to perform this duty. And despite this, he should be the captain of record? I just don't see it, sir!"

Boeteler was furious at the man's audacity, particularly because he had made this announcement in front of a crew from which full loyalty was required.

"Well Pines, that is the way it will be, and I expect full cooperation on this project or you will have to answer to the war department! Am I understood?"

"Yes sir!" Pines saluted, although the sneer changed to a menacing look which rested on the inventor.

February 17th, 1864

The man was screaming at him and nearly frothing at the mouth in anger. Moses Isaac couldn't believe his ears.

"I'll be darned if I let you pilot the ship! This is history in the making and no sinner Hebrew such as yourself will be the leader of this sacred mission!" With a stern gesture to the rest of the crew, he raised his voice even higher, even though it seemed like an impossible task. "Who is with me on this?!"

Nearly in unison... nearly, the crew raised their own voices to match their leader's, and with a strident yell, they howled in response, "Aye!"

Old Cairns was the only abstainer. He looked at Moses with pity in his yellowing eyes, spit at the ground, and began to walk off. Spinning on his heels, Cairns charged at Pines with the bellow of a mad bull. A great, meaty hand reached out and lifted the Lieutenant bodily from the dock by the neck.

"Now, you'll respect Moses, or by the Lord I'll pop your head off like the cork from a bottle!" the elderly man hissed through clenched teeth.

Pines gasped and wriggled as his face turned different shades.

Moses, completely out of character, raised his voice to such a degree as to be heard above the commotion now taking place on the dock, and shouted "Release him, Tom! You'll kill the man, and anyway, there must be some reason for this!"

"Only because you've said so Moses, otherwise I'd have throttled him a bit longer!" Cairns exclaimed as he tossed the trembling sailor to the ground like some toy doll. Stalking off towards his hill residence, Cairns looked back once more with an empathetic look at his friend, the inventor. The look quickly changed to malice as he glanced once more at Pines before he was gone.

Pines stood up shakily with the look of someone who had recently looked over the precipice of the edge, leading to the next world. In a moment, he had regained his composure and motioned to his crew to follow him.

Moses looked on in shock as sailor after sailor gave him angry looks as they climbed aboard his creation. When Lieutenant Pine had slipped through the hatch, he rose back up and gave the submarine's inventor an evil smile before ordering the craft into the harbor. There it sailed, or rather swam, into the pages of history, while trailing its torpedo[11] behind it.

All that work. All that effort, and he would never be part of its maiden voyage. There was only room for one commander in that hull, and Moses was not going to fill that role. All his dreams of heroically leading his incredible submarine to battle against the Union blockade squadron seemed dashed; the honor and glory that sprung up in his mind when working on this invaluable creation was now in tatters. He couldn't bear to watch any longer, so he buried his head in his hands and cried. What a pitiful looking figure standing there on the dock on that cold, misty morning.

Suddenly, a searing light lit the morning fog and was followed by an explosion that split the sky. Then, a low rumble pulsed through the water and soon after, a final shock wave radiated through the air, shaking the buildings that surrounded the harbor. The USS Houston, that giant boat with all the cannons on it, seemed to disappear; to be replaced by a black cloud of smoke that rose towards the sky before mushrooming out in a nearly perfect display of Biblical proportions, like fire and brimstone. Its magazine must have blown.

Moses uncovered his eyes and peered out over the water as had everyone close by. After a few moments, about half of the people went back about their business, cataloging this violent display of man's desire to demolish itself with all of the others they had witnessed in the last four years of America's Civil War. After another five minutes, the eccentric inventor was the only person still scanning the wave tops for a blue light that meant his ship was returning to its

---

[11] This refers to a mine, called a torpedo during the American Civil War which, unlike the torpedoes fired by modern submarines, contained no engine to move it towards its target.

home. The only thing present was the scent of the sea air, the caw of the gull, and the lifeboats rescuing the survivors of the blockade ship that gone up in the recent explosion.

The blue light never showed which meant the submarine would never return, and after half an hour its inventor turned his back on the water and shuffled back to his camp.

He had been saved yet again: This time, in a most awkward and surprising manner. That old, anti-Semitic feeling that was such an integral part of history had reared its head once more. It saved, rather than hurt him in this instance, as Moses was spared from being aboard the ill-fated submarine.

He said to himself, "It is indeed Abraham's Shield!"

The CSS Hunley. Moses' creation was based on the real life military submarine. It was originally produced privately and then commandeered for service by the Confederate navy.

Chromolithograph depicting the Battle of Hampton Roads

Ruins of the Tredegar Ironworks: where Moses had his own "works" for a while.

A LETTER HOME

This letter was found in the belongings of Hans Heller when he left this world in June of 1912. It was in a sealed envelope with just the words, "Letter from the war years," inscribed on it. It has been kept in its unopened state in the family for years. Recently, my Grandfather handed it down to me, which was approximately 100 years after it was first discovered. I thought it would be of some interest to the public, so here it lies. It has been edited only in the way of spelling and grammatical corrections. Other than those few changes, the content and order is exactly as it was initially written. My hope is that those who read it may learn something about the American Civil War that the textbooks don't teach you: specifically what it was like to be directly involved as a soldier. The fact that Hans tells quite an interesting story is just an added bonus.

Aaron Heller 2012

July 8, 1863

Dear Mother,

How are things back in Rochester? I miss you all terribly and cannot wait until I can see each of you again. Things are good here. We are well fed and we have new shoes and uniforms, which were sent by the gracious ladies of the north by some of their clubs, which donate these things to our cause regularly. I've been told they raise money for these supplies by baking and sewing and what not, but whichever way they happen to come, I am happy to have them.

I know I've been a bit remiss in keeping you and Tatty updated with my welfare, etc... All I can tell you in that regard is that I've been quite busy fighting this war. This last battle, Gettysburg, was perhaps the most intense I've been involved in up till now.

My division was in the thick of the fighting, and I've been doing some secret work which they tell me I am not at liberty to reveal just yet.

This is the first time I've been able to put pen to paper since the battle, even though it has been over for a few days. You probably know just as much or more about the main events that have occurred from the papers up there, but I have a story to tell that I can bet wasn't in any publication.

I'll just say that your son almost ended the war single handedly. You may read this and think that I am exaggerating, but I most certainly am not. The whole thing could have ended had I taken the shot, but I am getting a little ahead of myself. Perhaps I should begin from the beginning.

The date I believe, was the 30th of last month, and I was assigned to Buford's Cavalry Division doing some of my special work. We ran into what they tell me was Heth's Division while looking for supplies. These soldiers in rags who resemble scarecrows have quite a bit of fight in them, let me tell you. Looks can certainly be deceiving. Anyway, we ran into quite a few of them here and there, but then they all just randomly disappeared, only to return in larger numbers the very next day, which was July 1st.

During the first day of real fighting, I carried important orders from General Reynolds to General Meade as he was bringing up the main part of the army. I met him on the dusty roads leading into what would be the battlefield. The leader was surrounded by officers coming and going, so I couldn't deliver my message to him initially. That was until I stated rather emphatically that I had a letter from Reynolds himself.

One of Meade's aids brought me over to the General and I handed him the letter. After reading it, Meade looked off into the distance for several moments before looking back at me.

"Do you really think that the whole Southern Army is concentrating over there?"

I was just about to answer when another messenger rode up and announced that Reynolds was dead! Shot by some sniper as he was directing a charge. I was shocked!

I don't know if you've heard tell of the many exploits and heroism of General Reynolds, but you can believe me when I tell you that you have never met a braver or more capable commander in camp or field. He was always at the front, unlike some commanders, who lead from behind. He exposed himself to every danger and expected nothing from his men that he wouldn't do himself. This gained him the respect of all, and yet he was always careful in his planning and execution.

I rode back to the battle with a heavy heart for I felt close to the general, but I soon forgot all about it as I got caught in the retreat to Cemetery Ridge and the Round Tops. They are the two hills, one small and one large, that made up the left of our line. The firing was quite hot in all quarters of that field as we made our way to our very strong positions.

Later that night, Captain O'Keefe came to my tent and told me about a new mission he had for me. Usually, we went on these missions in pairs, but I have been working alone since Pat was killed during the Chancellorsville fight back in May.

What he had me do, I cannot say, and I don't want to worry you, dear mother, but I made it out safe and sound, so I guess I did my job well. I think I can tell you that I had to report on the Confederate troop movements from my vantage point, but anything else I cannot.

Despite the fact that Sickles was surprised in the Peach Orchard and we almost lost the Round Tops, I found a way to inform headquarters of an attack that Longstreet was launching, giving them enough time to send reinforcements.[12] And they arrived none too soon, I can tell you! That was a close shave if ever there was one!

After that, I spent the night in pretty comfortable quarters, although outdoors. I am a light sleeper as I'm sure you'll remember, but the exertions of the day had me played out.[13] I woke up to a furious cannonading from both sides sometime around 11 o'clock on the morning of the 3rd. The guns on the ridge burped and bucked as they threw their balls and shot at the

---

[12] See attached map.
[13] Slang term for the time; meaning exhausted.

other side. They were then answered by our side just as quickly! I have never seen such a spirited artillery duel before. Even what we did to the town of Fredericksburg[14] was nothing in comparison to this.

Then, all of a sudden everything just stopped and I could make out the long lines of southern infantry debouching from the woods as they made their way towards our men who were waiting on Cemetery Ridge.

It seemed the maddest thing in the world, those unprotected ragamuffins in their homespun garments, heading towards the blue lines of some of the bravest men in the world who just happened to be armed to the teeth and full of fury! Yet, they did it! I must admit that these southern boys have more pluck than you can imagine. It's going to take us a long time to beat them; that I can attest to!

As they kept marching, our boys opened up on them, and soon after, the grey lines began to falter. About twenty men would be mowed down by the converging fire of artillery and musketry, and the marches would draw closer to one another. It was certainly glorious, but it was still a slaughter.

A small contingent of southerners even reached our lines, but they were shot or captured to a man. I've heard that most of their commanders were killed during the charge. The rest that were still standing began a steady retreat under fire until they reached the woods where they had originally emerged from.

From my vantage point, I was able to watch all of this as it unfolded. I also saw Robert E. Lee himself come up on his bay charger to the retreating masses once they were in the woods. He kept saying things like, "It's my fault. All my fault. Brave men must stand together now and do our duty," and so forth.

This is when it became really interesting. I had the perfect shot on him! I raised my rifle and took a bead on him. He was riding tall on his great grey horse. There was no way for me to miss, especially from such a close distance! I could have ended the Rebellion right then and there with one pull of my trigger. It would have been so easy!

And then, it happened! I don't know if I've told you about my friend Levy, and I don't have the time now, but let's say he is one of Abraham's children like we are. The two of us shared some interesting moments together, even though we were on opposite sides of this war.

Levy rode his own horse right smack in my line of fire! I guess I could have shot both him and Lee clean through, but I just couldn't bring myself to do it. General Lee got a reprieve because of Levy.

---

[14] One of the most criticized actions of the war was the bombardment referred to here by Hans. The entire town of Fredericksburg was decimated in preparation of a Union assault on the town and the hills beyond it. Civilians were trapped in the town during the tremendous shelling and many perished then or were injured.

After a few moments, my position was compromised and I barely escaped by the skin of my teeth, so I wasn't able to wait around for a second chance at taking the shot.

I think I am getting a little long for a letter, so I'll just end this by saying that I love and miss you, Tatty, and my brothers and sisters back home. I hope this war ends soon so we can be together again.

Your loving son,

Hans

P.S. Maybe I will get that second chance at a shot on Lee after all!

Major General George G. Meade

General John F. Reynolds - Killed on the first day of Gettysburg.

Depiction of Pickett's Charge. Print of the painting "Hancock at Gettysburg" by Thure de Thulstrup Restoration by Adam Cuerden.

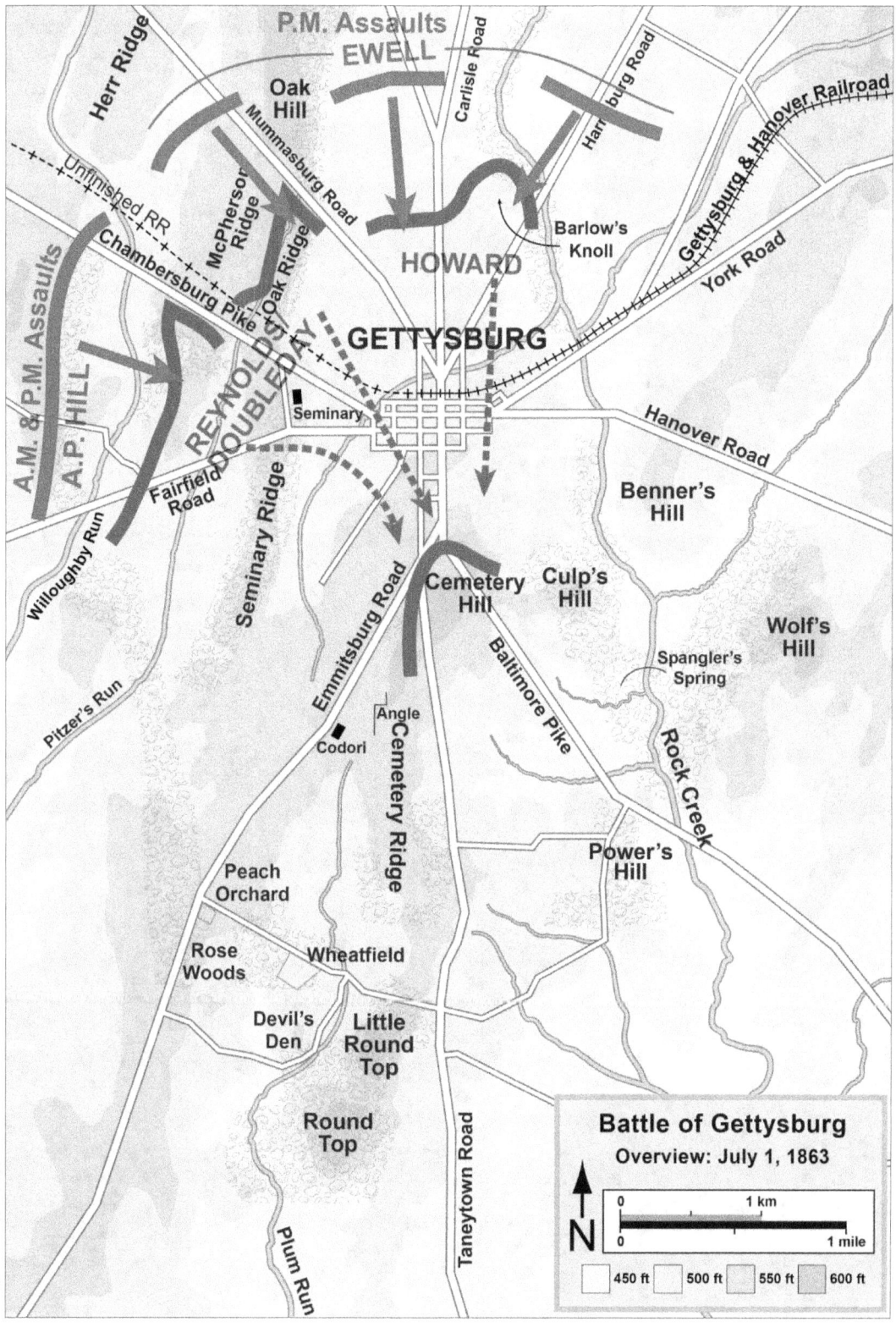

Herr Ridge

P.M. Assaults
EWELL

Carlisle Road

Hanover Railroad

Oak
Hill

Mummasburg Road

Harrisburg Road

Gettysburg & Hanover Railroad

Unfinished RR

McPherson Ridge

Oak Ridge

Barlow's
Knoll

HOWARD

York Road

A.M. & P.M. Assaults

Chambersburg Pike

REYNOLDS

DOUBLEDAY

A.P. HILL

GETTYSBURG

Seminary

Hanover Road

Fairfield
Road

Seminary Ridge

Willoughby Run

Emmitsburg Road

Benner's
Hill

Cemetery
Hill

Culp's
Hill

Wolf's
Hill

Pitzer's Run

Spangler's
Spring

Angle

Codori

Cemetery Ridge

Baltimore Pike

Rock Creek

Peach
Orchard

Power's
Hill

Rose
Woods

Wheatfield

Devil's
Den

Little
Round
Top

Round
Top

Taneytown Road

Plum Run

Battle of Gettysburg

Overview: July 1, 1863

N

| 0 | | 1 km |
| 0 | | 1 mile |

| 450 ft | 500 ft | 550 ft | 600 ft |

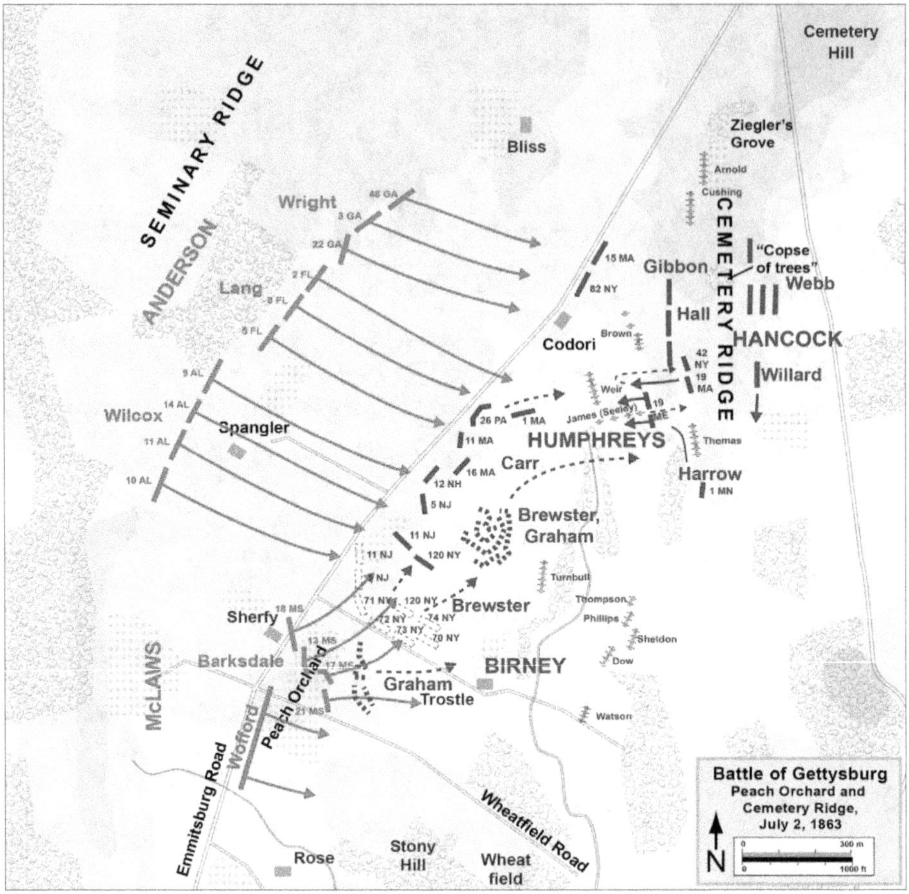

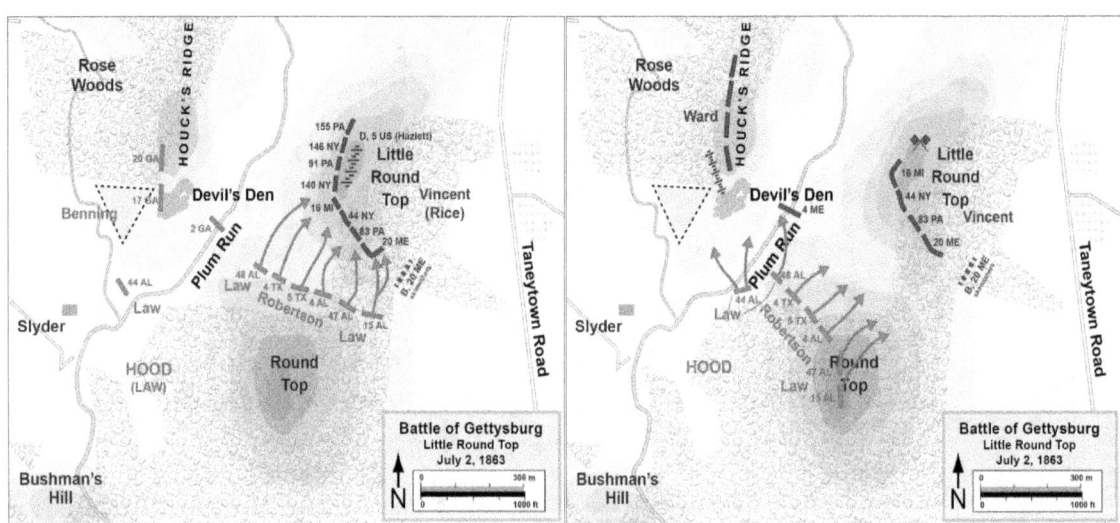

Battle of Gettysburg
Peach Orchard and Cemetery Ridge, July 2, 1863
SEMINARY RIDGE
CEMETERY RIDGE
Cemetery Hill
Ziegler's Grove
Bliss
Codori
Spangler
Sherfy
Trostle
Rose
Stony Hill
Wheat field
Peach Orchard
Emmitsburg Road
Wheatfield Road
ANDERSON
McLAWS
Wright
Lang
Wilcox
Barksdale
Wofford
HANCOCK
Gibbon
Hall
Webb
Willard
Harrow
HUMPHREYS
Carr
Brewster, Graham
Brewster
BIRNEY
Graham
"Copse of trees"
N
300 m
1000 ft

Battle of Gettysburg
Little Round Top
July 2, 1863
Rose Woods
HOUCK'S RIDGE
Devil's Den
Benning
Plum Run
Little Round Top
Vincent (Rice)
Round Top
Slyder
HOOD (LAW)
Law
Robertson
Bushman's Hill
Taneytown Road
N
300 m
1000 ft

Battle of Gettysburg
Little Round Top
July 2, 1863
Rose Woods
HOUCK'S RIDGE
Ward
Devil's Den
Plum Run
Little Round Top
Vincent
Round Top
Slyder
HOOD
Law
Robertson
Bushman's Hill
Taneytown Road
N
300 m
1000 ft

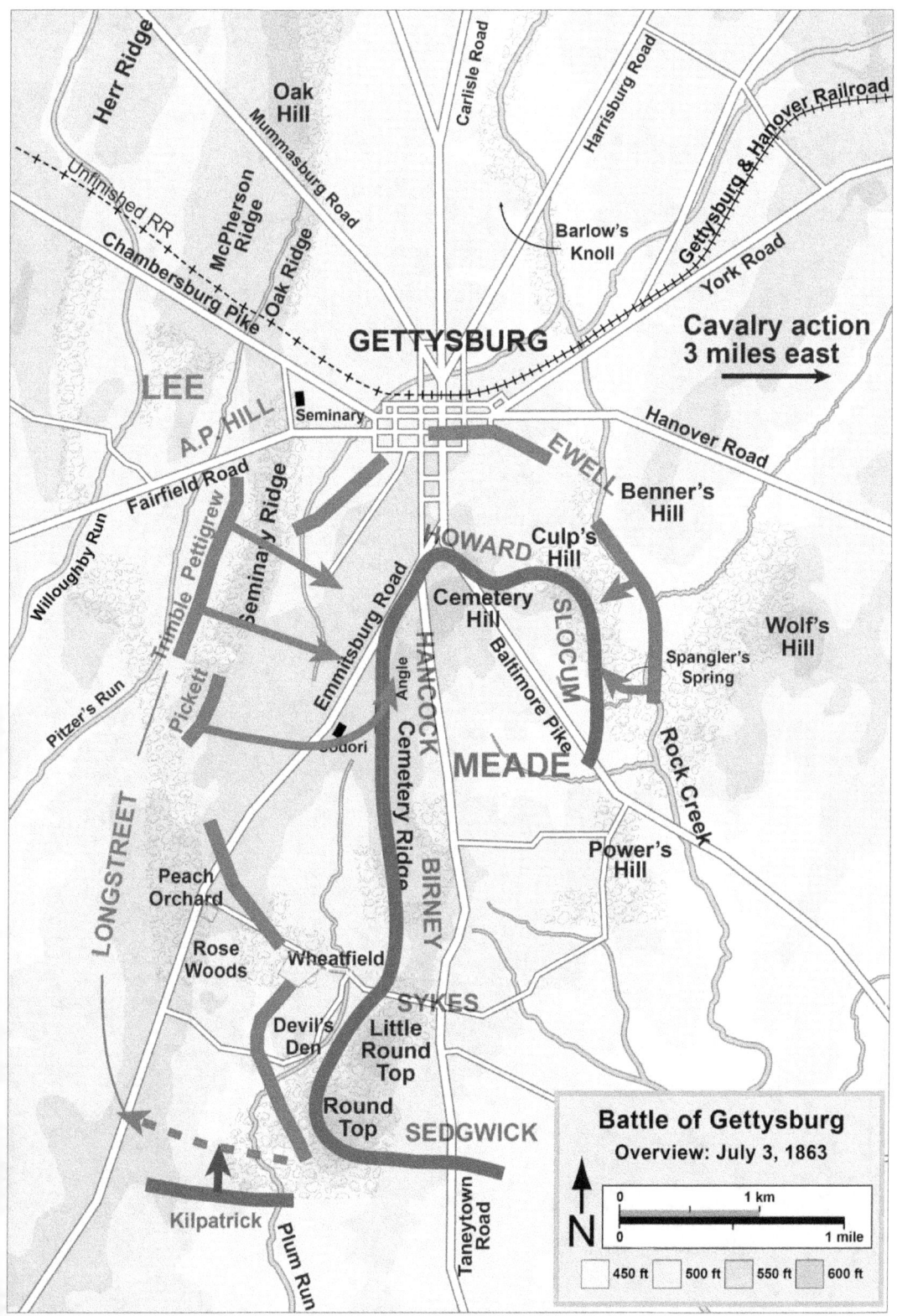

Herr Ridge

Oak Hill

Mummasburg Road

McPherson Ridge

Oak Ridge

Carlisle Road

Harrisburg Road

Gettysburg & Hanover Railroad

Unfinished RR

Chambersburg Pike

Barlow's Knoll

York Road

GETTYSBURG

Cavalry action
3 miles east

LEE

A.P. HILL

Seminary

Fairfield Road

Willoughby Run

Trimble Pettigrew

Seminary Ridge

EWELL

Hanover Road

Benner's Hill

HOWARD

Culp's Hill

Cemetery Hill

SLOCUM

Wolf's Hill

Spangler's Spring

Emmitsburg Road

Angle

HANCOCK

Cemetery Ridge

Baltimore Pike

Pitzer's Run

Pickett

Codori

MEADE

Rock Creek

LONGSTREET

Peach Orchard

BIRNEY

Power's Hill

Rose Woods

Wheatfield

SYKES

Devil's Den

Little Round Top

Round Top

SEDGWICK

Kilpatrick

Plum Run

Taneytown Road

Battle of Gettysburg
Overview: July 3, 1863

N

0   1 km
0   1 mile

450 ft   500 ft   550 ft   600 ft

THE BOUQUET

A day like June 21st, 1864 is rare indeed. The cool breeze and bright blue skies made one feel as if all would be right in the world. Such was not an easy feat considering the state of the country at the time.

At 6am, Levy found himself seated on a rock next to the pond on his family's plantation. It was a favorite pastime of his to trek out to the spot to think. He gazed out over the still water as the birds called to each other and the smell of fresh grass and dew wafted through the coolness of the morning. Today was the big day, and yet despite his best efforts, he was unable to feel the happiness that should have been his due.

Levy was getting married to his childhood sweetheart, Hannah. He loved her as much as life itself. His every thought was tinged with her image. Whether he was in the midst of heated combat or during a time of quiet thinking in camp, his every thought was directed towards the upcoming marriage to his love.

She was his best friend, and had been since they were little children running through the waving fields surrounding the plantation. They had caught frogs together in the very pond he now sat next to, and dreamed children's dreams together while pointing out shapes in the white clouds that drifted high above the hill. Their friendship had changed to love over the years: one of God's miracles.

Furthermore, Hannah was Levy's compliment in so many ways. Where he was thoughtful, she was playful. He was conventional, and she was imaginative. He preferred to sit and talk quietly at the edge of parties, and she loved to dance. They were opposites, but rather than repelling each other, an attraction was present.

After the wedding, Levy would be heading back to the front as his services to General Lee were considered invaluable. The facts that a war was convulsing the country and that the Union Army Juggernaut was bearing down on Richmond from all sides caused Levy tremendous worry about the future. What type of world would he be bringing children into?

To add another degree of anxiety to things, he would probably never see his "brother" Hans from up north again. Levy had just been reading a piece about a daring Union raid to sink one of the Confederacy's last remaining ironclad ships. It had been carried out and the Southern boat had sunk in the most daring manner. According to the article, which now hung listlessly from his hand, every Union raider had been captured or killed. Those captured were to be tried and hung, as likely as not. The real troubling thing was that this action had Hans' touch written all over it! The way it was accomplished and the risk involved spoke reminiscent of his friend's involvement. Hans was as good as gone if he wasn't in the next world already.

Most of Levy's closest relatives and friends would not be present for the big day. Robert E. Lee would never have missed his wedding during peacetime. In fact, he had promised that he would be in attendance if the war allowed him to; unfortunately, an unexpected threat rose up to thwart such a possibility. General Grant had stolen a march on old man Lee and was now poised to cut off the only supply line to the capital, which was the railroad that lead from

Petersburg to Richmond, the capital of the Confederacy. It was the city's lifeline, and it was also the Southern Army's main method of obtaining supplies. If the connection was cut, the downfall of Richmond and the Confederacy would surely follow in a matter of days. Hence, most of the military family that would have attended the wedding were not able to be there, and that included the commanding general.

The idea that the beautiful plantation, which had been his childhood home, might fall into Yankee hands any day was just another painful jab to his heart. His father had already left this world for the next, and his brother had not been heard from in over a year. He was out there with John Bell Hood somewhere near Atlanta, or at least it was hoped he was. Despite the joyous day that lingered about, the world still seemed to be crashing down around him.

As his thoughts joined the mist swirling above the pond, he felt his body grow lighter and lighter until he was just air. Perhaps he could grasp his new wife and fly to a new world. Hashem would be there to help; of that he was sure. God's plans were a mystery to him, but he was confident that there was indeed a plan, a reason for it all.

Then, his mother softly touched his shoulder.

"Levy. Levy. We have to get ready. We can't be late now."

"Mother, of course," he murmured as his soul returned to his body. "I'll be along shortly."

Levy took one last glance at the peaceful surroundings and then made his way back to the house slowly, trudging up the wooden chip path in the wake of his mother.

In the Jewish tradition, the day of a wedding is a day of reflection and prayer. God listens to a bride and groom's prayers more intently, and people will ask them to pray on their behalf. Whether it is for children, sustenance or health, every supplication is given to the couple under the wedding tent, or chupa, as it is referred to in Hebrew.

It was such a prayer that Levy's mother implored him to make.

"Please Levy, I know you are thinking about many, many things on this very special day, and I am very happy for you, but please keep your brother in your prayers. We have not..." she started, but paused briefly as she sobbed and let a tear fall from her cheek. "We have not heard from him in over a year and I am just worried sick. You'll pray then, won't you?"

"Of course. Of course I will. I long to see him too! We will! I know that sooner than later he'll be home! You've got to trust in Hashem and he'll answer our prayers. I know it!"

"Yes. Yes, of course he will. Oh, but enough crying! This is a happy, happy day! Let's get to the shul right away!"

As they rode in their wagon, which was being piloted by their faithful servant, Otis, towards the synagogue, it was clear from the empty fields and burnt homes that the war was nearing its dreadful conclusion. A few slaves poked their heads from the ruins and watched as the carriage made its way through the rutted lanes, the mud oftentimes hushing the sound of the wheels. It was a melancholy ride.

Glancing back at his mother, Levy thought of happier times, like when his family had still been whole. He knew that his incredibly caring father, who was the ideal southern patriarch, would be beaming with pride from heaven, but it would still be better if he were there in person. Who would walk him down the aisle towards the bridal canopy? It had been done that way for hundreds of years, and now Levy was without an escort.

Arriving at the synagogue, the guests, although numerous, did not qualify as a crowd in the usual sense. Knots of guests, mostly older men, women, and children milled about at the entrance to Richmond's main synagogue, Beth Shalom.

The Bride's family had been there for some time, and in the tradition of the Jews of America, had kept their daughter in a separate room when the groom entered. They smiled when Levy walked in, and Hannah's father embraced him as he would have done to his own son.

"Levy, I know your father would be proud to see you now; all grown up!"

"Yes, thank you Mr. Cohn. I know he would be." The thought was intensely painful, but he knew that his soon-to-be father-in-law had the best intentions in mind.

The Rabbi entered from his study, placing both of his arms on Levy's shoulders, smiling a broad, warm smile. "Levy, I am absolutely thrilled to be here with you today. I recall your bris," the Rabbi said with a wink, referring to the ritual circumcision that Jewish males have performed on them on the eighth day of life. "And now, now you are grown and marrying one of the most eligible daughters in our community. I am beaming with pride!"

Before the actual ceremony, the groom was lead to see his new bride, who was waiting in another room of the old building. The attendees gathered to witness the first time Levy would see his veiled bride on his wedding day.

He entered the hall, accompanied by his soon-to-be father-in-law, and began to walk across the wooden-floored hall. A violin played a traditional Jewish melody and the guests became quiet. Each step brought him closer to his bride and he could hardly contain a smile of thanks to the One Above.

Levy's mother and Hannah's mother flanked his intended, her beautiful eyes shining brightly from beneath the veil. Her eyes locked with Levy's as the shroud was lifted. Now, as their gaze met, it became clear to Levy that everything before that day had lead up to that very moment.

Levy let the veil drop and was led away to another room to read what is known as the Tanaim, or "conditions," as the word is translated in literal terms. The ancient text of the wedding agreement, set up over 1500 years before by the Rabbis of Israel and Babylon in order to protect the wife in case things did not work out, was read to the groom. After acknowledging the conditions, Levy signed his Hebrew name to the document in front of two witnesses. His mother and Hannah's mother then held a dish wrapped in a napkin and smashed it to the delight of the guests. Now, all that remained was the actual wedding ceremony.

As the music played softly, Levy walked slowly towards the Chupa, with his mother on one side and his Uncle Moses, who was well-groomed for once, on the other. After reaching the canopy, Levy turned to watch his bride as she walked down the aisle towards him.

Upon reaching the slightly raised section where the poles of the Chupa were placed, the bride, trailed by her mother and Levy's mother, circuited Levy seven times.

The Rabbi then stepped in, giving specific instructions to Levy as he proceeded to hand him the ring without a gem, as per the Talmud, and uttered the words that have bound man to wife countless times over many years amongst the Jewish people: "Hari at Mikudeshes Li"[15]

Seven blessings later, and Levy broke the glass. He leaped down from the platform arm in arm with his wife, full of joy. Amongst the cheering and clapping, his heart was frozen momentarily by a strange, unexpected feeling. He'd had that feeling twice before: once in that trench during the battle of Chancellorsville, and the other was after that glorious, but futile charge on the third day of Gettysburg. The great Confederate division composed of some of the finest in that army was decimated, the remnants washing back towards their lines, lapping around their profound, in-defeat leader, Robert E. Lee. Levy had ridden out to see if he could be of service to his general when the feeling of protection came over him and the words, "Abraham's shield" popped into his consciousness.

Now, even as everyone smiled and danced, Levy couldn't shake the odd feeling. He noticed his wife was looking at him with a look of concern on her face; for a wife, just made or not, has the ability to look into the heart of her husband and see if things are amiss.

"What is it, Levy?" she whispered in his ear.

"It's nothing, darling. It's an old feeling I've had before, that's all. It's a good thing, I think."

That speech, spoken as it was in hushed tones, didn't seem to do much to assuage the unsettling feeling which Hannah seemed to have just then.

Suddenly, from the midst of the wedding party, a man with his brim pulled low and clothed in the black grab of a southern planter, stepped forward and thrust a bouquet into Hannah's hands. He turned as quickly as he appeared and was gone.

---

[15] Translates loosely as "Behold, you are betrothed to me."

The couple craned their necks and struggled to pick the stranger out amongst the other guests without any luck. They hadn't noticed him before, and now it seemed that he had vanished into thin air.

Levy glanced at the bouquet which his wife was now holding, and noticed a note sticking out from amongst the delicate yellow blooms. The 2-inch note was scrawled in pen on a yellowing background, likely ripped from some field manual or something. It read:

"Mazel Tov, Levy! I'm sorry I couldn't remain to celebrate with you!

Your Brother,

Hans"

THE BATTLE OF PETERSBURG V? APRIL 2?? 1865.

A Currier and Ives depiction of a battle during the Siege of Petersburg

Confederate entrenchments during the siege of Petersburg

"Ruins in Richmond" Damage to Richmond, Virginia from the American Civil War. Albumen print.

WHERE IT ALL BELONGS

Chapter 1

The inky black silence of a winter night in the Shenandoah Valley was pierced by the shuffle of several feet treading over the frozen ground. As the party crested the top of the hill, the torches spread a flickering circle of light about their feet. Long shadows cast themselves hauntingly over the stunted trees that lined the path. The man who appeared to be the leader paused momentarily, glanced around, and making a decision to continue, proceeded down the opposite slope. The rest followed cautiously, being careful not to stumble or upset the wagon, which was being pulled by a pair of Sorrel horses that were straining under the heavy burden.

This leader was of more than average height, and less than average weight, although a certain energy and strength could be discerned in his movements, and his stride exemplified confidence to the extreme. His black moustache drooped over a strong chin and was met by raven sideburns extending from the sides of his bony face.

"Come, hurry yourselves! We must move faster!" he exhorted the crew. "No slacking now!"

Fear was present on every countenance as they did their master's bidding: marching along in the frosty, torch-lit mountain country. A light snow began to fall from the Heavens, making the way even more treacherous.

Stooping at the bottom of a depression, the tall man, whose name was Otis Brians, held his hand up as a signal for the party to stop.

"It's here! Dig here!"

One of the men stepped forward with a shovel, and struck the hard ground with the tip. Some dirt and ice was displaced, but the ground was nearly frozen solid.

Pushing his servant to the ground, Brians grabbed the shovel from him with a hiss and began digging, making a deep indentation. "Like this you fool! Must I do it myself?" he snarled.

Several others jumped at these words and brought their own shovels and pick axes to bear on the hard earth.

Perkins, the man who had been thrown to the ground, rose to his feet, rubbing his leg where he had fallen on it. He grimaced and picked up the shovel, which had been unceremoniously tossed on the ground near him by Brians, and got to work with the others.

A cavern began to open up under the constant rain of shovels and a torch was thrust into the hole. The light glinted off strange crystal formations and tooth-like protuberances, which gave the impression of the maw of some giant monster.

"This is it," said Otis Brians through clenched teeth. "The rope, now!"

Perkins stepped forward with a long curl of rope, unraveling it and tying it to a tree. The other end was dropped into the cavity.

The lanky form of Brians lowered itself via the hempen rope into the cavern, first followed by the others, one by one, until only the horses and a lone sentry remained above ground.

Blowing into his hands to warm them, he peered intently at the walls.

"Here is the path!" he exclaimed, and proceeded down a dripping passageway.

"I don't like it one bit! It strikes the fear into me, it does!" a servant named Grady whispered to his companion.

"Aye, it does!" he replied.

"What was that!?" hissed Brians tuning on his heel, the torch light illuminating his fiendish countenance. "You'll do well to be quiet!" he said, touching the pistol at his side menacingly. "We must hurry!"

A few moments later he found a spot hidden behind a crag jutting from the wall in a cavern illuminated by the eerie reflection of torches on the crystalline pillar that dominated the middle of the room.

"Here, place it here!"

With that, they dragged forward a gigantic chest and heaved it into the crevice created by the protrusion of rock and cave wall.

"Now, cover it with rubble and be quick with it!" their master yelled, brandishing his gun.

After the work was done, Brians ascended the rope, hand over hand with a surprising agility, given his five and forty years.

As he reached the opening, he dragged himself over the edge and looked down.

With a wicked grin, he reached into his belt and pulled forth his pistol. When his eyes met Perkins' gaze, he pulled the trigger.

The look of shock was frozen on Perkins' features as the bullet entered just below his left cheek. It exited with great force, taking much of the brain and bone fragments with it, spraying the other servants' upturned faces with the material that was formerly their associate. His hands convulsed and he hung to the rope for a few seconds before falling into the hands of his comrades in the cavern below.

Brians then unsheathed his Bowie knife, its 10-inch blade glinting in the light from the torches, and sliced the rope with one swift movement.

Curses and screams shot from the hole as their master shoveled dirt and rocks into it. With great effort, he rolled a gigantic rock he had placed near the spot some days earlier, over the opening and sat down on it while the muffled cries from below became fainter and fainter.

When the last noises had ceased, Otis rubbed his hands together, lifted his face skyward, and proclaimed to the stars, "My treasure is hidden from all eyes!" Then he laughed; an evil laugh that split the dark night, which would have made a person's hair stand on end; that is, if anyone else had been alive to hear it.

Chapter 2

Hans had just picked up his load of newspapers from the distributor before he looked out on the cold Rochester streets with disdain. Another day of hawking this tripe in below-freezing weather was not high on his list of things he'd want to be doing right now.

The steam from fresh horse droppings and pedestrians' breath joined in a fog that hung over the cobblestones and then disappeared into the gray air. During the summer, it was bearable, with temperatures rarely peaking past eighty-five. The winter on the southern shore of Lake Ontario, one the five great lakes that straddle the border between Canada and the US, was anything but mild. Typically, two or more feet of snow would cover the ground with the thermometer barely above zero degrees for weeks at a time.

Into this frozen cityscape, Hans tucked his papers under his arm and walked with his head down and shoulders bunched. The wind bit at any part of exposed skin, which in Hans' case, was the tip of his nose, cheeks, and any of the holes that lined his shoes and threadbare clothing. A trail of red blotches stood stark against the white snow where Hans had walked. It was a cold winter indeed.

Arriving home after his long day of selling, or rather, not selling newspapers, Hans dropped his satchel on the wooden floor boards and slumped into the rickety chair next to the stove that took up a large portion of the kitchen in the tumbledown house on the corner of Boardman Street. He held his head in his hands and shivered.

It felt good to be out of the cold, and holding up his hands to the stove erased some of the chill from his bones.

"Who is it now?" called a voice from the side room.

"Tatty,[16] it's me. I'm back." Hans responded to his father's question.

"Hmm. What have you brought then?"

Rolling his eyes to the cracked ceiling, he sighed before answering. "Not much. Fifty cents I think."

"Not much, but it's what Hashem[17] wanted to give us today!"

Hans leapt from his chair and rushed into his father's presence; the frustration apparent on his handsome features.

---

[16] Yiddish for "Daddy"
[17] God - Literally translates to "The Name" in Hebrew.

"Father! You say that, but look around! We're starving, and when we run out of what little money we have, the bank will take this house! All you say is Hashem will take care of it! It doesn't seem like it right now!"

"Trust in God, my boy! He will come through!"

"What are you talking about? Mother cannot care for the little ones and work at the same time! And I can only bring in so much with the newspaper, and you're not able to walk anymore! Praying will not help any of us! I can't take this existence anymore!"

And with that, he banged out of the room and back into the frigid night air.

"Hashem will help you, my son. You shall see before you are much older," Hans' father said to the empty space where his son had just been.

Hans nearly tripped over the pile of newspapers as he ran from the house. Cursing under his breath, he glanced back at the stumbling block of papers. The headline caught his attention.

The evening edition had in bold letters plastered across its yellow face, the following headline: "UNION DISSOLVED!"

What was this? He stooped and picked up the paper, reading the rest of the reprint from a South Carolina paper. In the near future it would change the lives of millions of people, but for now, it would change to Hans' life in ways he could never imagine.

Chapter 3

It had been a difficult month of May for the Union forces in the Shenandoah Valley. Jackson, or as he was referred to by his troops, Old Blue Light, was wreaking havoc on the armies of three supposedly accomplished Northern generals. The Confederate army, which consisted of all strata of Southern society from aristocratic planters to backwoods subsistence farmers, had repeatedly bloodied the nose of a superior foe with a combination of audacious tactics and sheer willpower.

This was a fine morning in the valley, and the weather was perfect. A scene more astounding in its beauty could hardly be hoped for. Pink-tinged flowers fringed the deep brown branches of the Dogwood trees. The green shoots of new growth and promise were everywhere as the dew clung to blades of grass with a pleasant coolness. Aromas of flowers, earth, and clear air hung there for the taking. The entire scene looked as if it had been painted by a master hand.

It was into this tranquil scene that Hans trotted atop his great black horse, Canandaigua, named for that beautiful gash in the earth filled with water where Hans' grandfather had his farm. He, because of his skill as a horseman, which he gained while helping at the upstate NY farm, had been assigned to the 5th New York Cavalry brigade and served as a scout. This assignment offered him everything his life in Rochester lacked: freedom, excitement, and a sense of importance that was sorely missing. If he failed at his job, his brigade, or perhaps the entire army itself, could be immersed in peril. These missions brought with them a certain degree of danger that Hans found intoxicating in the extreme.

It was on such a mission that he found himself that lovely spring day. He had just crested a hill and began his descent into a steep ravine when a twig snapped somewhere up ahead.

Stopping in his tracks, he pushed the horse toward the fringe of trees and waited in relative protection to see what would happen next.

It was a few moments until the source of the noise made itself known. Tobias Athens, a blond-haired member of the same cavalry regiment as Hans and a fellow scout, rode into a clearing at the bottom of the ravine. Looking around and satisfying himself that he was alone, he climbed from his horse and began fumbling with something in his saddlebag. Finding the object he was searching for and glancing about again, he removed it from its hiding place. It was a small shovel of the type used by miners in the western portion of Virginia[18].

He began to knock the handle into the earth until he seemingly found what he was searching for, and after swinging the shovel around, he began to dig.

Hans watched all of this from his place of concealment with interest. When Tobias began to dig, his unknown observer, unable to resist any longer, ventured forth with a call.

"Hey there, Tobias! What are you doing there?"

Spinning on his heel with a look of fear mixed with guilt perhaps, Tobias instinctively hid his digging implement behind his back.

"Who is it now?" he exclaimed, before his expression relaxed upon seeing Hans.

"What are you doing there, Tobias?" Hans repeated.

"Oh, nothing. Just uh... just digging for uhm... water, you know? It collects at the bottom of these holes, if you weren't aware."

"Yes, but we've got plenty of water around here." Hans said with a sweeping gesture. "Why would you be searching so hard for it?" He was already suspicious, and this conversation was doing nothing to allay his doubts.

"Just in case, you know..." and then he changed the subject. "Hans, what were *you* doing in these parts?"

"Colonel Smith has me checking for tracks of any marauders that might have been hanging around the area. Someone heard Morgan was about here, so we're looking for signs. If any of us find any, we are to report back and get a posse together and go after 'em!"

"Sounds like fun. I was doing the same thing pretty much, but I decided to take a sidetrack and look for water here."

"Yes... water. Well, I best keep looking. I'll be seeing you."

"Yes, you too, Hans!"

And with that they waived and rode off in separate directions, both glancing back to make sure that the other had disappeared from view.

---

[18] Until 1863 there was no West Virginia. The residents were fiercely loyal to the Union and were rewarded with their own state, which comprised the mountainous region to the north and west of what is now Virginia proper. It is (or was) a place of great mineral wealth and for years supported a hearty, if crude population who extracted the coal and other material from the mines by the sweat of their brow.

Chapter 4

As the sun set on the beautiful valley scene, the shadows chased rose-colored lights, and a cool breeze was rustling the leaves on the otherwise tranquil trees. Then, a dark silhouette appeared between the trunks. It was a man leading a horse. He carefully stepped out from the forest, but remained close in case he needed its protection in the near future. Shading his eyes from the intense bands of light cast by the sun, he looked out on the quietude.

The man waited until the rosy hues of the sky changed to purples, and then to black, with a twinkling diamond necklace of stars clear and bright above his head. He then ventured down the slope until he reached the spot where he and Hans had run into each other previously.

Lighting a match, the handsome countenance of Tobias Athens became visible. His long blond hair hung in ringlets about his shoulders and his moustache was trimmed perfectly. He pulled a dark lamp[19] from his tunic and lit it, causing a small cone of light to project out a few feet in front of him.

Tobias found the large rock he had been searching for earlier when his plan was temporarily interrupted by Hans earlier that day. With some effort, he pushed it towards the woods, continuing on for several feet. Underneath the stone, the ground was a different color; the dull color of clay.

He pulled out his shovel and began to throw the chunks of soft red earth aside.

Shortly after, the dirt began to become looser and looser and the clods of earth gave way at last, tumbling into a shaft about 3 feet across. A hot column of acrid air shot up from the cavern. This was the spot. Tobias glanced around once again to make sure that no one was watching him. Satisfied that he was alone, he rubbed his hands together and tied a rope to the nearest tree. Putting on his cavalry gloves, he grasped the rope and lowered himself in.

Why was he here? A strong influence was at work and there was only one thing that could move the young cavalry lieutenant to place himself in such a precarious situation; miles from his command and in the close vicinity of vicious enemy brigands. Tobias knew the answer very well: Treasure.

---

[19] Portable lamp with a built in shade

It had been during the battle of Manassas,[20] and Stonewall's famous stand on Henry House Hill had turned the Union or Northern tide from victory to defeat in a matter of half an hour. The whistle of .58 caliber bullets was frightening in the extreme for most of the men who had never seen battle, or "The Elephant," as combat was referred to in the common vernacular of both armies.

Tobias was one of those men, and he had nearly dropped from exhaustion before *even* getting to the battle. During the march on that Sunday, July 21st 1861, along dusty roads and over the crests of rolling hills, he had sweated through his army-issued tunic and mopped the perspiration from his brow with his regulation cap.

Upon reaching the battlefield, he went to stack his arms along with everyone else and sat down to consume his rations. The time was now about 1pm. They had been marching since 4 in the morning and the rest was much appreciated.

Suddenly, their sergeant, a man by the name of Eyers, yelled out, "Okay, men! Up and grab your rifles! March! Forward, like we practiced!"

Tobias and his fellow soldiers jumped to their feet and ran for their stacked arms. Grabbing their weapons, they sprinted back into line and awaited orders.

The shot and shell from the Confederate cannons fell about them, digging 20 yard trenches where they touched down, flinging dirt and debris in all directions. A scream would pierce the air as an unlucky soldier was flung through it like a ragdoll from the impact. Still, the men stood straight, looking forward and not flinching; not wanting to be the coward who ran to save his own hide. So, for what seemed like an eternity, they all waited under the hot sun, sucking in dust and blinking.

Then, the command came. First a bugle some ways off sounded and was taken up by others, and then the army began to move straight ahead as a collective. Initially, the step was measured and the commanders walked in front holding their swords high for their men to see.

Random rifle shots began to pepper the advancing troops with the commanders groaning and then falling to the ground to be replaced by their subordinates who grabbed their swords from the ground and marched forward, perhaps to be leveled by a wicked 58-caliber projectile.

The grim determination that became a hallmark of the Union soldier could already be seen during this event, the first major battle of the Civil War, and even though soldiers fell with grievous wounds, the command pushed forward.

---

[20] There were in fact two battles of Manassas. It was known in the South as Bull Run as the South had different naming conventions for battles. They usually named the battle after some natural geographical feature while the North named them after the nearest towns, crossroads, etc... For example: Sharpsburg (name of the town) and Antietam (name of the creek the battle was fought near). At the time of the narrative, the second battle had not yet occurred.

When the Northern troops reached the hill where the Confederate brigade of Thomas J. "Stonewall" Jackson was perched, the order broke, and then each soldier charged in at a run using whatever tall grass or logs they could for momentary cover before darting forward again.

From the corner of his eyes, Tobias saw what he thought were horsemen approaching at a gallop, but it was hard to tell what they were and which side they were on in the melee of cursing, smoke, and the deadly rain of bullets.

Out of the fog of war emerged the horseman known as Jeb Stuart, crashing into the Northern flank. Slashing and stabbing, the horsemen waded into the infantry with devastating effect. It was much like the wars of medieval times where one soldier would pick an opponent and they would fight to the death.

Amidst the chaos, Tobias picked his man: a tall, thin man on a jet black horse who had made short work of the first two opponents he had encountered. Raising his rifle, he took aim from about a yard away, and fired. The shot nearly lifted the rider out of his saddle, but he held on, grimacing in agony as the horse circled back. Though he looked to be in a lot of pain, the horseman did not fall from his mount. Instead, he clung on, his face twisting in agony as the horse slowly trotted towards the woods. Tobias saw the effect of his shot and decided to give chase on foot, knowing the horse wouldn't go too far whilst still dragging the body.

Reaching the woods, Tobias realized that he had hit his target and wounded him quite severely. The telltale sign was a puddle of what appeared to be blood, but it was thick and almost black. Stooping down, he was able to discern the bloodied trail that would lead up to the injured man and his horse. It was clear as day and could only mean one thing: the man was near his end; else he would have covered his tracks.

Coming around a bend into a clearing, he saw what he had expected to. Sure enough, there stood the horse with its rider bent over the saddle, and by all appearances, he was lifeless. Tobias checked around before stepping into the midday sunlight. The air was alive with bluebottles, mosquitoes, and others of their kind, buzzing about relentlessly. He saw no one as he approached the cavalryman cautiously, his rifle at the ready.

Just then, he noticed the man move. The injured soldier, who still dangled from the horse, grunted and turned towards his would-be antagonist. His face was seamed with evil wrinkles and a pair of piercing eyes that regained some of their luster upon seeing another human face. The drooping mustache must have been stylish in the South. Now, as it dripped blood, it gave the impression of drooping moss or willows.

"Aye. It's you. The one who shot me," he said weakly as the blood trickled from the corner of his mouth. He coughed loudly and then spoke softly, straining his voice as the words escaped. "Can you get me off this horse? It pains me to sit like this."

"Yes, it was I who shot you."

Tobias reached up and gently lowered the man to the ground. He set him down in the tall grass and used his hat as a pillow. Tobias looked nervously about and then asked, "Is there anything I can do to help ease your pain? It's a shame to see you suffer. We may be on opposite sides of this war, but we are still men."

A year later, the realization that his decision would prove to be a poor one would catch up to him. If this scene had played out at that time, Tobias would have walked away and left the man in pain, or at the most, he would have just put him out of his misery. This was of course, was long before he had been through the hells of war. At this early stage however, he still clung onto faith in humanity and was truly concerned about his fellow man.

"Just a bit of whiskey, if you will. It's in my saddlebag; right over there," he nodded towards the pocket, too weak to point.

Reaching in cautiously, Tobias pulled out a silver flask and held it to the dying man's lips.

"Ah, that's much better," the man gasped. "I will probably not make it, but I'll make you an offer for being so kind. If I live..." Without warning, he coughed violently, spitting blood into the air. "If I live," he continued, "you'll split it with me. If not, it's all yours since I'll not need it."

"Wh...What are you talking about?"

"A treasure, my boy! Such as you've never seen in your life! But..." he hesitated, as another cough roared through his lungs. You must swear now that if I live, you'll return half of it to me!"

Not seeing much in the way of a choice, and since he hadn't much to lose, Tobias nodded in agreement. "Sure, I'll swear."

"Okay then," the man said, gasping for breath and clutching at his chest where the bullet had pierced his lung. "My name is Brians and I have more money to my name than the hairs on your head! I put some of it away for safekeeping in a secret spot: in the Shenandoah Valley, where I'm from. The money is close to a certain creek. You'll know it by the twisted tree at the Valley pike, south of Winchester..." The man proceeded to give a detailed account of how to find the exact spot where the cave that hid his treasure was located.

The young soldier listened with rapt attention to all that was told to him. Greed had always been a bit of an issue with Tobias in the past, and the prospect of a windfall such as this one had piqued his interest.

"I've got it."

"So you have," Brians whispered. Then, his eyes rolled back in his head and the life that he had been clinging onto, left him.

Tobias slowly stood up, repeating to himself what he had just heard. He looked around furtively to make sure no one had heard him, and then he scampered off into the woods, taking the silver flask with him.

The next morning, after joining the defeated Union army in its retreat, he sat down in his tent and etched the instructions on the backside of his wide riding belt.

Six months later, he found himself to be a cavalryman in the Northern army that was pursuing Jackson and his band of soldiers in the Shenandoah Valley. He knew it would be the perfect opportunity to see if the man's story was true. And it was.

Chapter 5

The splash of his boots on the wet stone floor brought Tobias out of his fugue. A small stream wound its way along the ground of the cavern. Peering into the darkness, he beheld the giant stone pillars which appeared in the light of his torch as the teeth of some gigantic beast, a cold mist emanating from its maw. A crypt-like atmosphere hung heavy in the air and his footsteps echoed ominously through the chilled, empty space.

Shaking off the feelings of danger, he focused on the task at hand. Where was the treasure? Where would Brians have hidden it?

A thin, white object thrust into a crevice on the wall caught his attention. It was if it had been set up as a marker, pointing down the passage. Holding out the torch for a closer look, he quickly became aware that many more bones protruded from the stone walls throughout the cavern; they seemed to be placed at various forks in the tunnel.

So intent was Tobias on following the signs that he nearly tripped over the hempen rope that was stretched across the floor. Bending down, he cautiously tugged on it. Suddenly, from somewhere in the darkness, an axe swung down and embedded itself into the wall where Tobias' head would have been had he still been standing upright. The place was sewn with traps! Brians had not mentioned this, however. He had either forgotten in his injured state, or he never intended to have his treasure fall into another's hands and had tricked Tobias into meeting his doom in some sort of twisted, underground revenge.

Moving even more cautiously, Tobias kept his eyes moving up and down the walls, floors, and ceilings, on the lookout for more pitfalls.

He nearly headed back but couldn't resist the promise of treasure which he knew was waiting somewhere deep within the belly of the earth.

Stepping cautiously across some polished stones, he trembled when one of them unexpectedly sunk into the ground with a click. Somehow, he managed to press himself against the wall just as a shotgun blast reverberated in the closed space; nearly taking his head clean off.

"This place is just full of surprises," Tobias said under his breath as he recovered from the shock.

After picking his way along the passage a bit further, he came to the place described by Brians as 'the spot that marks the treasure.' It was an amphitheater-like space with a tremendous rock formation in the general shape of a sheepdog. There was an alcove towards the back, which was covered in part by a waterfall.

Ducking beneath the falling water and being careful not to extinguish his torch, Tobias knocked on the walls until he felt something hollow. This was the spot!

He placed his torch against the wall and began to scratch at the surface with his clasp knife. The rocks began to fall away under the chiseling until a smallish space opened up. He worked faster until all the stones were cleared and an undersized wooden chest was revealed.

Removing his gloves, Tobias grasped it with both hands and gave it a mighty heave. Small pebbles trickled to the floor and it began to jiggle. Another pull and it finally came away from its spot. He scoffed at how heavy it was for its size.

Tobias then placed it on the floor and examined it closely. There was a heavy hasp in the shape of a skull with a hole for the key in one of the eyes.

"Nice touch," he said to himself as he thrust a thin chisel into the slot. With a crack that echoed over and through the cave, the lock snapped and gave way.

With intense anticipation coursing through his veins, he lifted the lid. What greeted his eyes in the light of his torch was more magnificent than he had expected or hoped for. The box was full of the most beautiful jewels and pearls he had ever seen. Diamonds of the first water, rubies of incredible size, and shining blue sapphires filled the container nearly to the top.

Tobias then set about removing the box's contents. After spending over an hour counting, he was finally done. There were 40 diamonds over a carat in size, 23 emeralds, and 45 rubies, along with hundreds of other various jewels. 16 beautifully shaped pearls were set in a crown of sorts, which itself was fashioned of very fine gold; so pure that it bent when touched too roughly.

"There must be nearly a million here!" he said smiling gleefully. "Too bad you won't be in on this Brians! Ah well!" he exclaimed as he began carefully packing the riches back into the chest.

"I can't take this with me now," he thought to himself. "I'll hide it again right here, but I'll take just this one with me now," he muttered aloud as he plucked a gem of brilliance out. Tobias then removed his wide riding belt, and with a piece of burning ember, he etched into it, a map of exactly where he had hidden the treasure. When he emerged from the cave, dawn was nearly breaking with hints of lightening in the east. After covering the hole with a large rock, he laughed heartily to himself before heading for his horse. The treasure had been concealed for a second time, and now it was all his.

Chapter 6

It was some three months later that Tobias found himself fighting alongside Hans during the Second Battle of Manassas. Their cavalry detachment was assigned to what was thought to be on the flank of Jackson's II corps. It was in fact, the very center point where both corps of the Southern Army converged.

Pope, the pompous general in charge of the newly created Army of Virginia,[21] was badly mistaken in his assertion that the army now facing him was merely a detachment and sacrificed thousands of good soldiers in an attempt to overrun a railroad cut,[22] which was essentially entrenchments, and provided excellent cover for the defenders.

In addition to this mistake, Pope did not realize that General Robert E. Lee had sprung a trap where two of the main branches of his army would come together like a vise, crushing the Northern Army in between its two sides. His army was defeated very soundly, to say the least, losing nearly 11,000 troops by most estimates, to the Confederacy's 8,500 or so men killed and wounded.

Hans had just emptied his cartridge of his new Spencer repeating rifle towards the line of smoke puffs, which represented the enemy entrenchments, and was reloading when Tobias came riding past, shouting that the US flag, which was carried into battle as a rallying point by every regiment, was down. Someone needed to carry it forward and he was headed towards it.

Hans watched as his dashing compatriot rode headlong into the fray, dodging bayonet thrusts and clubbed muskets to grasp the flag and charge ahead, shouting, "Long live the Union!"

It was indeed an impressive site, and both sides stopped fighting to watch the gallant act. Well, almost everyone stopped. A young private, Silas Merner by name, on the Confederate side, saw what was happening and became incensed by the audacity of the act. He lifted his gun and took aim at the blond, long- haired cavalryman from the North. Pulling his slouch hat down to shade his eyes from the sun, he ran forward, leaping over a fallen soldier and smacked Tobias on the back of his head with his rifle.

---

[21] Not to be confused with the "Army of Northern Virginia," which was the principle Southern Army during the Civil War. The Northern army had a brief life which effectively ended with the defeat at the Second Battle of Manassas, or Bull Run as it was known in the Northern States.
[22] Area cut out of the ground with the intention of laying down railroad tracks.

Tobias grunted and turned towards his attacker. He stayed conscious just long enough to see his foe smiling at him with a wicked grin on his face, before he lost his balance and fell sideways from his horse.

Silas was slightly shocked by his actions, and his first thought was to turn and run. On second thought, he walked over to the northerner in the fancy boots and began to drag him by the shoulders towards his own lines. Perhaps, he thought, he would be promoted for capturing a Yankee officer.

Chapter 7

The first thing Tobias felt was a searing pain in the side of his head. It seemed like he had been falling; falling into an abyss that lasted for days. In truth he had been unconscious for about half an hour, but the mind can play tricks on you, especially after being clobbered by a rifle butt. His eyes began to flicker, and then suddenly, they fell open.

A bright light, brighter than the sun, was a lamp in the hospital next to his cot. The next thing that assaulted his senses was the stench: the smell of rotting flesh, blood, and alcohol. This was in the days before modern medicine had discovered germs and antiseptics, and doctors kept their blood-stained saws in velvet boxes. Needless to say, a hospital tent was not a pleasant place to be and certainly not an enemy tent as was the case with poor Tobias.

The screams of the amputees came next, and then the groans of the recently operated on followed, or those struggling with a bullet wound still. Last, came the sweat. A cold sweat had soaked through the thin sheet he was lying on and he was cold; colder perhaps, than he had ever been before. He began shivering and looked around.

A stern looking sentry, Silas, was seated by his bedside.

"You're awake then, Yankee."

"I uh, where am I?" sputtered Tobias.

"Well," Silas replied, looking around slowly. "It seems like you're in a hospital tent behind Lee's lines." Then, he turned back to Tobias with a wicked grin. "Scared, are ya?" He pushed his face close and shouted, "You should be!" The yellow teeth and rank breath caused a wave of nausea to well up in the captive's stomach. "Once you're fully awake, we'll just mosey on in to the general and find out what you know..." he said, grinning once more.

"Oh, no. I'm just a low down cavalry private. I don't know anything. Really."

"Well that's the first lie you told, you Yankee scum! I see by your coat you are a lieutenant.

Tobias couldn't argue with *that,* so he just fell back into his cot and waited to see what would happen next.

Silas pushed Tobias roughly out of the hospital tent and along the path leading to Longstreet's tent. Once inside Longstreet's tent, Silas thrust him with little gentleness into a chair.

"You just wait thar Yankee!"

"Doesn't look like I have a choice," mumbled Tobias.

"What'd you say, you Yankee varmint?!" Silas yelled, putting his face quite close again to that of his captive.

Turning to the side to avoid the foulness of the situation, Tobias replied quietly. "I said, it is quite clear who is in charge."

Straightening up again, the southerner seemed satisfied. "Well now, that's better." He then wandered out of the tent to look for his superior.

General Longstreet was in consultation with his commanders, a field glass[23] in his hands. He was built like a tree trunk with a muscular physique, and a reddish, flowing beard which showed no traces of grey. Slow and methodical in preparation, he hit like a sledgehammer when he launched an attack. He was the perfect foil for Jackson's near impetuosity in battle. Lee had called him his "Old Warhorse," and Longstreet had yet to let his superior down.

"I tell you General, we've got 'em this time. That fellow Pope is as confused as a cat in a room full of rocking chairs!" his adjutant was saying as they pored over the maps spread on a camp table.

"I understand, Jenkins," the general was saying, "but I never like to attack with one shoe off. I will recommend that we reconnoiter in force before we proceed. There may be more of them than we think, and McClellan[24] may be coming up on our flank."

This conversation was interrupted by Major Cobbs, who was in charge of the prisoners. He had been standing amongst the officers clustered around the general.

He was a lanky, sandy haired Texan of about 35 years, with a handlebar mustache. It was hard to find a being that was at once gregarious and greedy like Cobbs. People loved him for his personality and loathed him for his avarice. He had a propensity for taking everything that wasn't tied down, which, as the officer in charge of prisoners, was profitable in the extreme. He ran a side business acquiring and selling captured soldiers' equipment and weaponry.

"General Longstreet, I have captured a cavalry officer (taking credit that wasn't exactly his) and he may have some information we could use. Would you like to personally interrogate him? He has just awoken from his temporary incapacitation," Cobbs finished with a smile.

"Well then, Major, let us see the prisoner and then we can finish our discussion, as what he says may be pertinent to our current topic."

They marched as a group into the hospital tent. Longstreet sat down in the camp chair that was being placed next to the prisoner's cot by a nurse, and let out a loud grunt.

---

[23] A small telescope held in one hand.
[24] This is not the place for an in depth review of the battle but it should be noted that General McClellan was just finishing up his unsuccessful Peninsula campaign and was ordered to save Pope's skin. Because of several complicated political and selfish reasons, he did not offer his full support. Longstreet could not know this and his concerns were perfectly valid.

"Thank you, nurse," he said, nodding to the attendant. He then turned towards the prisoner with a serious look on his face.

"Now, son, as you can see, you've been captured by your enemy. We in the south know how to treat our prisoners well, but I must ask that you cooperate fully so we can in good conscious exchange you[25] at the next opportunity. Do you understand me?"

Tobias was surprised to be in the presence of such an important Southern general and didn't respond immediately.

"Do you understand, son?"

"Ye...Ye...Yes, I do," he stammered. "But I can't compromise my fellows. Even if I knew something, which... which I don't!"

Tobias realized he may have said too much, but it was already too late to take his words back.

"Hmm," Longstreet sneered, looking even more intently at the captive. "I do believe you can tell us a little bit more than you are letting on about what's happening on the other side. I have no time for games, however. Will you talk straight or not?"

He responded with a shake of his head and then looked away from the general.

Longstreet sighed and stood up, straightening his huge frame. He glanced over his shoulder at Cobbs, who was grinning like a wolf in a sheep pen.

"Well major, he's all yours now. See if you can make him talk," and with that, the general ducked out of the hospital tent and into the waning sun of the afternoon. He was followed by the group of officers.

Cobbs walked over to the prisoner, who now had a look of fear in his eyes, although he did his best to hide it. Still grinning, Cobbs bent down and looked the prisoner over like a vulture examining the carcass he had found lying there for the taking.

"Well now, my friend. Let's talk," he intoned as he sat down on the same camp chair that Longstreet had occupied a few minutes prior.

---

[25] Both sides would regularly exchange soldiers who had been captured. General Ulysses S. Grant stopped the practice in 1864 after becoming the commanding general of all of the Union armies. This allowed the Union, with its superior manpower, to win what had essentially had become a war of attrition at the end.

Chapter 8

It was a perfect day in Rochester, NY. The sun was shining and the breeze blew in tantalizingly from Lake Ontario. The populace was all smiles; all except for a family in the rundown house on Boardman Street.

"Heshy! Please, you must eat something! Heshy!"

The old man turned slowly in his chair. His ashen face and fallen cheeks displayed a lack of nutrition as clearly as if the word 'starving' had been etched into his forehead.

"Mother, save it for the children. I'll be fine. Really, I will. Hashem knows what He is doing."

"Heshy, if you don't eat, you'll further burden this family with your funeral, *Chas V'Shalom*[26]!"

"Well, I've been thinking really. We have to find a way to bring in some money..."

"With what? Hans is off fighting and you're not in any shape to work. The children need me here. The only thing we've got is this house!" The lady of the house was shouting as she wandered around the dining room making such a speech. "All we've got is this old house!"

"Yes," Hans' father replied. "Exactly what I was thinking."

---

[26] Literally "Pity and Peace" in Hebrew. Colloquially it means, "God Forbid."

Chapter 9

Tobias felt like he had just been dragged through the streets of his hometown by a horse. In truth, he had almost been. The way Cobbs had treated him was just short of how one would treat an old dog that had just bitten its master. But, he preferred not to think about it as he trudged down the dirt track, dragging the foot that hurt him most. Instead, he focused on how he was going to escape. Rations, if you could call them that, were handed out once a day and consisted of green corn and a handful of flour. It was just enough to keep a prisoner alive, but not much more.

There was some fiendish calculation in the amount the captives received. If the prisoner was not able to lift his head from hunger, he didn't stand much chance of getting away. Even if the prisoner escaped, he'd be in no shape to fight for a while. It was as simple as that, really.

There were some other deprivations and mistreatment meted out to prisoners, including lack of sleep, degradation, and psychological tortures. Even getting shot while trying to escape held more promise than Tobias' current predicament.

Needless to say, all of his belongings had been taken away, including his favorite pair of riding boots, his gloves, his Colt pistol, and his shiny Springfield rifle. Nothing was left but his pants, shirt, and belt, and he was not given a new pair of shoes. The soldiers in the South couldn't even obtain them for themselves, and a prisoner's podiatry was not a priority to the Confederate Army, to say the least.

So, Tobias shuffled along, feet bleeding, spirit bent, bruised and battered and without enough to eat for several miles. He had lost count of the towns he had passed and no longer had any clue where he was. Finally, his sight left him. Everything turned black, and he lay himself down on the road, waiting to die.

A guard approached him and gave him a kick in the side. Tobias grunted, but did not move. "Captain!" the soldier yelled to a mounted officer riding nearby. "What should we do? This one ain't moving!"

"Won't move, huh?" he asked, while turning in his saddle to face the supplicant. "Shoot him and leave him there as a warning to others who would do the same."

"Are you sure, sir? I mean, we could just throw him in one of the wagons and get him looked after when we reach a hospital."

The captain reined in his horse and stopped in his tracks. He leaned down and looked at the soldier for a few seconds. Then, in a quiet voice, which was more menacing than any amount of raised tones could have been, he said, "Did I ask for your opinion? Do you see what's on my collar? I'm the captain, and you are not. So you will do as *I* say. Now, shoot him and move on, or you'll be marching along with the other prisoners. Do you understand?"

"Yes, Captain Wirz," he gulped.

The guard, whose name does not matter much, but was David O'Toole, turned and raised his rifle. He mouthed the words, "I'm sorry," and started to pull the trigger.

"Wait!" a voice screamed as the clatter of a horse's hooves could be heard barreling up the road.

As the dust cleared, a slight figure clad in an impeccably tailored, gray officer's uniform reigned in his horse in front of Captain Wirz. The insignia showed him to be a mere lieutenant, but his dress meant he was more than his rank indicated.

Captain Wirz knew him well. He'd had his orders meddled with before by this very same junior officer. To make matters worse, he was a Jew. These people felt that for some reason they held the moral high ground and were always swooping in to save the less fortunate or oppressed. They were heavily involved in the abolitionist movement,[27] which was, in the opinion of Wirz, one of the major reasons they were fighting this blasted war in the first place.

All reasons aside, this Jew named Levy had the most annoying of habits: he was always in good humor.

"I have news from General Lee! You are to bring the prisoners forward at a slower pace until…"he said, stopping mid-sentence. After acknowledging what was going to be the imminent demise of a prisoner, he exclaimed, "What are you doing here? Hold fire!" Levy screamed at the private about to end the prisoner's life. Then, spinning to the captain, he spoke. "Captain Wirz! You have direct orders from Robert E. Lee to *not* execute prisoners on these marches! I don't wish to report this, so let's load this poor northern boy into a wagon and drop him at the nearest hospital."

"Levy…" Captain Wirz began, with more than a touch of exasperation in his voice. "I'll not have him shot, but I cannot be burdened with a prisoner that cannot walk. If I were to carry him, I'd have to carry every one of them that throws themselves down," he said while making a sweeping gesture towards the long line of prisoners trudging up the dust road.

"If you would like, we can take this up with the general. Up to you, Captain," Levy replied with a smile that did not convey good feelings.

Wirz attempted to keep his composure, but his expression belied hatred and something more; perhaps it was a desire for revenge.

---

[27] It must be noted that there were several key religious and secular figures in the Southern Jewish community who supported slavery as it is mention very clearly in the Bible. Rabbi Morris Jacob Raphall, himself a Northerner, supported slavery vehemently and engaged in a famous debate with Rabbi David Einhorn during the war.

"Okay then, Lieutenant, we'll do it your way," he replied evenly, and then to O'Toole, the soldier who had just about ended the prisoner's life, he said, "Please place the prisoner in that wagon there and drop him at the nearest hospital."

Satisfied, Levy took to the reins of his horse and galloped off to where he had come from. Wirz watched as he disappeared into the distance, grinning evilly the entire time. This would not be the end of it; not if he had anything to say about the matter.

Chapter 10

Tobias had been borne along in the wagon for a day or so. Captain Wirz had made sure that it was no comfortable ride for him, placing a living pig in the wagon along with him. He got used to the smell quite quickly, but the darn animal was constantly squealing and stepping on him.

At the end of the following day, they reached a small outpost somewhere in North Carolina, which had a hospital. The prisoner was speedily revived and tossed unceremoniously from the wagon at the entrance to the tent.

Tobias stood shakily. He had regained a little strength from the ride, and could see again as he had received a double ration from O'Toole when the Captain was not looking.

Captain Wirz sneered at the wobbly prisoner and whispered in Tobias' ear from horseback. "You got lucky this time, but I'll be sure to see you again when you're well," and giving the prisoner a kick with his boot that sent him sprawling in the mud which covered the field, he rode off to rejoin the column of prisoners.

O'Toole glanced back with a look of pity as Tobias struggled to his feet again. Then, a guard ran over, grabbed him by the elbow, and led him into the hospital tent. O'Toole gave the reins a twitch, sending the wagon off after Captain Wirz.

After being nursed back to health by the good graces of the nurses, Tobias was told by the guard who had picked him up from the mud that he heard that he would be paroled, meaning exchanged for a Southern soldier of similar rank, and then sent home.

This sent his heart leaping from his chest. Finally, he would be going back to the home and hearth of his family! All he could think of as he wandered around the camp under the watchful eyes of the guards, was seeing his mother and father again.

Eventually, the day came when an officer rode up and handed one of the guards a note. Looking at it, the guard made his way over to where Tobias was standing.

"Come with me!" he exclaimed curtly.

Was this it? Was he going home? Was this hellish war over for him?

"Present your hands!" the guard commanded. When Tobias complied, the guard proceeded to wrap them with heavy rope. After he was sure that his prisoner could no longer free himself, the guard tossed the rope to the officer on horseback who saluted the guard and pulled the prisoner along with him, away from the hospital.

Tobias nearly trotted along beside him, so excited that he was going home. They rounded a corner and Tobias skidded to a dead stop, the rope that connected him to the guard becoming taught. There, in the middle of the rode, seated atop a great black charger was someone he knew all too well.

"Well hello there, old friend! It's so nice to see you again!" Cobbs smiled his sinister smile beneath his drooping, sandy mustache as he greeted him.

Chapter 11

Upon seeing his former torturer sitting atop his horse in a nonchalant manner, Tobias realized that he might not be getting paroled so quickly. The first words spoken by Cobb confirmed it.

"Tobias! You look well! Much better than the last time we met. I've got an idea, and I think you won't be going home that quickly after all. Captain Wirz and I are old pals and we talked about you and your situation."

A lump began to grow in the back of his throat.

"So," continued Major Cobbs, "I have a proposal for you. It's not really a proposal as much as it is a choice you have to make."

"Wh...What is it?" Tobias was barely able to get the words out. This couldn't be good.

"Well, I think you'll like the idea actually. You'll definitely like it more than being shot and thrown in a ditch at least." And with that, Cobbs' hand fell to his holster where his colt pistol rested.

"How can I decide if I don't know what it is you're asking me to do?"

"That's easily cleared up. I need you to let me know where other prisoners have hidden their valuables. It's an untapped mine. They hide the stuff they want to keep, and sometimes they take their secrets with them to uh, well... to where soldiers go when they've been 'mustered out of the service,' if you know what I mean."

Tobias did know what he meant, and he had a hard time not believing he would be joining those soldiers soon.

Cobbs continued, "Anyway, I know there's thousands I'm not getting and I've got to get it! They won't very well tell me, but they may tell another prisoner. That's where you come in. Understand?"

He did. As low and degrading as this proposition seemed to him, something in it struck a chord with Tobias. That greed, that lust for acquisition which lay dormant during his time as a prisoner was awakened, and he smiled to himself ever so slightly.

Cobbs, catching the smile that flitted across the young cavalryman's face, slapped his thigh with an open palm. "I knew it from the moment I saw you!" he exclaimed. "You're a greedy son of a gun just like me! You and I are gonna get along just fine."
Cobbs stretched out his hand and Tobias grasped it, thinking that this could work out well after all.

Chapter 12

The year 1862 passed into history, and there were no signs that the war would end anytime soon. A good number of prisoners had been exchanged or paroled and gone home, never to fight again. Some of those left in custody bounced around from southern prison camp to prison camp, becoming thinner each time until they were not much more than walking skeletons.

Tobias was not one of those types of prisoner. He had not wasted away, and his working relationship with Cobbs had ensured that he was well fed and protected to some degree. He was always spirited in amongst the other prisoners at night and then was "shot" for some offense in nearby woods so that no one ever suspected that he was anything other than a prisoner. He was also given, at least promised at any rate, a share of the spoils from his nefarious conduct.

Cobbs became quite wealthy with the help of his Trojan prisoner. Things seemed as if they would stay that way for some time, but then in the winter of 1863/1864, Ulysses S. Grant was called from the West to be General in Chief of all of the vast multitudes that were the Union Armies. The tide of war began to change, and the death knell of the Confederacy could be heard by anyone who wished to hear it. There was one other change that led to events which caused the curious partnership between Cobbs the Major and Tobias the prisoner, to come to an abrupt end.

After the massacre at Fort Pillow, in which a certain cavalry general named Nathan Bedford Forrest captured the place and then slaughtered all of the African American soldiers instead of taking them prisoner, Grant determined not to exchange any more prisoners until black prisoners were treated the same way as white prisoners. The Confederacy declined, and prisoner swaps ceased, except in rare cases, until the end of the war. That meant that there would be more and more prisoners, which in turn meant more opportunities for the team of Tobias and Cobbs. A windfall if ever there was one.

It also meant more and larger prisons, and then came along Andersonville. That hideous, disease-ridden hole was where the team met its end, and Captain, now Major, Wirz[28] again.

Its stockade enclosed a fetid swamp, and from the moment the camp opened, it became clear that this was not like any other prison. Captain Wirz immediately instituted new rules

---

[28] Major Wirz was captured after the war and executed for the hand he had in the deaths of over 13,000 prisoners. He was the only Confederate tried and convicted of war crimes for his actions during the war.

which included the infamous 'Dead Line.' This was a thin fence approximately 19 feet from the outer stockade walls. Any prisoner showing an inclination to approach the walls, or even reaching the line, was shot dead without warning by the guards in towers. All in all, there were very few less unpleasant places that existed anywhere on earth in 1864.

Tobias was thrust in amongst the other prisoners, and there was very little Cobbs could do to protect him. Soon enough, Tobias was lying stricken and dying in a tent along with 30 other prisoners. The realization pushed its way into his fevered mind that he may not make it through the war. On the other hand, if he did, he may never be able to collect the treasure that was waiting for him, especially after the tumult that might result from governments being restructured. Who knew who would be in charge and which soldiers might be patrolling the areas? He knew it would be better to get the treasure out and safe before the war was over. But who could he trust to help him do so?

Cobbs was as close as anyone he could put his finger on that might help, so he requested a private audience with the Major to supposedly reveal Union secrets he had been hiding from his captors.

He was carried to Cobbs in a litter, being too weak to walk, and was unceremoniously dumped on the dirt ground of the Major's cabin.

Cobbs straightened himself up in his camp bed and glanced curiously at his petitioner, giving no indication of recognition. He stood and motioned for the guards who had brought the prisoner, Tobias, to leave them alone and then sat back down.

"Well…" he began, "How can I help you?"

Tobias was terribly incensed by the fact that his "partner" pretended not to recognize him. He struggled to sit up and began in a weak voice that was little more than a whisper.

"It's a fine thing for you to leave me to rot in this hell hole! And then to act as if you don't know me and I'm not your problem anymore! Why if I had the will I could make it very hot for you, you know!"

Cobbs leapt from his bed like a tiger while pulling a knife from under his bed covers. At the same time he grasped Tobias by the throat and held the 7-inch blade to his cheek.

"I don't think you'd do that now, would you?" he hissed through his yellow teeth. "Not if you want to keep your head where it is, that is."

Tobias grimaced and prepared to meet his maker. He couldn't prevent himself from shaking and turned a sweaty, malicious grin towards his tormentor with a look of defiance.

"I didn't think so," Cobbs said, dropping his prisoner to the dirt floor. He then straightened up to his full height. His chest was rising and falling in his fury and a wicked gleam in his eye betrayed the beast within. Then, as suddenly as his anger exploded, he was back to his old, jovial self.

"So, what can I do for you?"

"I've come to make you a deal. I am not sure I can trust you, but I've got nothing…" he said, bursting into a fit of coughing.

When he regained his composure after a moment, he continued. "I've got nothing to lose. I will make you an offer that will make you richer than you ever thought possible. I have a treasure that would have made Solomon himself jump! I can tell you where it is."
Cobbs was interested now, but he maintained his obnoxious smile, not showing any hint of desire to continue the conversation further. Tobias knew this man though, and he saw by the way Cobbs stood that he had gotten him interested in the treasure.

Chapter 13

"Well! Go on then! Tell me where it is!" Cobbs nearly shouted in his excitement. This was after 30 seconds or so of silence from Tobias. It was like high stakes poker, and Tobias was playing his hand with a deft touch.

"Not so quick. I need some assurances first."

"Okay." Cobbs calmed down a bit before he spoke next. "What is it you want, and I'll see what I can do?"

"First, if you are successful in getting the treasure, you will come and get me out of this hell."

"You know I can't guarantee that, Tobias."

"But you must! All you have to do is arrange for my transfer and I'll do the rest. There is no way I can escape, not with the death line over there." and he shrugged and pushed his head towards his left shoulder.

"Hmm... I think we can discuss that."

"Okay, so that's the first thing. The next is that we split the treasure between the two of us."

"Less any expenses I incur in getting said treasure, of course?"

"Of course. I also want my situation improved here a bit. Perhaps make me a prisoner guard or something. For the time though, I'll take a good hospital bed and food. You'll arrange that?"

"Yes, that is something I can do. Now, let's get on with the secret!"

"Not so fast! Lastly, once we meet up again, we'll shake hands and go our separate ways. No partnerships or anything of the sort. If they find out what we did up 'til now, we'll both lose our freedom."

"All right, you've got yourself a deal!"

"Now, you must swear this on a Bible before I tell you, or I'll quit this place."

Cobbs didn't have much of a problem with this as he didn't really place too much weight on religious matters. Besides in his eyes, his former partner wasn't exactly a pious man himself so he didn't see any harm in it.

"Sure then. Have you got a Bible?" he asked with an impish grin.

"As a matter of fact, no... but, you've got to find one or the secret gets buried with me!"

"Calm down! I'll get one from the fanatic captain who resides in the next tent over. Don't go anywhere!" he couldn't help giggling a little as it was quite clear that Tobias was not going anywhere, anytime soon in his current condition.

He returned within a few minutes, holding a rather large blue, covered Bible, and swore the most solemn vows he would never keep. Satisfied, Tobias removed his belt and proceeded to explain how to use the map he had scratched into it. Cobbs got back up to his feet when he was entirely clear on the matter.

"Well," Tobias exclaimed, "I wish us both luck in your quest!"

"Yes, thank you. Now I'll just get, ahem… the guards to take you to the hospital. Then, he shouted out of the tent flap, "Guards! Come and retrieve the prisoner! Take him back to where you got him from with an extra kick for me!"

Tobias was startled when he heard that and began screaming. "What? Our deal! Our deal! You can't just go back on your word!"

"Watch me!" he sneered, turning to the Guards. "Don't believe a word this crazy enemy says! He has lost his head and should be put back with the lunatics next to the stream."

"Why you piece of filth! I can't…" Tobias' speech dissolved into an unintelligible stream of gibberish as his anger got the better of him, and then he was carried away by the guards. Still kicking and screaming all the while.

Cobbs turned, and rubbing his hands together with thoughts of riches, returned to his tent to study the belt's map.

Chapter 14

Major Robert Cobbs had just pulled himself from the hole he had dug half an hour earlier. He stood and dusted himself off, breathing in the fresh night air of the Shenandoah Valley. Now that the real work was over, he was able to relax.

The treasure had been exactly where Tobias had said it would be. The cave itself was quite a wonder, and the depression where it was located was actually an indentation in the side of a larger hill left by some glacier thousands of years before. The ceilings in the cave were over thirty feet high in some places, and a spectacular maze of stalactites and stalagmites in various shades poked into the space at odd angles. There was one natural structure that actually resembled a lion, but of rock. Tobias had mentioned none of this, but Cobbs was more of an artistic man, and the beauty of the place amazed him continually as the torchlight glinted off the glistening walls of the cavern.

Having counted the jewels and gold, Cobbs had stuffed his coat with a goodly portion of it, perhaps $100,000 worth. Despite his good fortune, there was one catch: because there was such a tremendous amount of treasure, one man alone would never be able to cart it all off at once. He thought it better to wait until the war was over, where he could then return with a crew in which he trusted, or more likely payoff, when things were quieter. He hid the rest of the valuables in a different spot on the off chance that anyone else came looking for them.

Just now, he had to concentrate on getting out of the South with as much money as possible, but this would be no easy task. He had asked for leave,[29] and instead of heading home, he headed for the Shenandoah Valley and its riches.

The Valley itself was a hotbed of military activity in the fall of 1864. General Philip Sheridan of the Union was pursuing Confederate General Early down the Valley, drubbing Early's forces every chance they got. Scouts and guerilla bands were everywhere and had lately taken up the practice of shooting prisoners instead of being encumbered by them.

This was not exactly the best place to find oneself without a very good reason.

Cobbs mounted his horse and gave a glance back at the place he just emerged from. He had covered his tracks well, and there was little chance anyone would find the hole in passing. Even if one were looking for it, they still might not see it unless they were to look very closely. With heavy pockets due to the gold and jewels, Cobbs wheeled his indistinct brown horse around and headed north.

---

[29] Time off from active duty allotted for officers.

Chapter 15

Robert Cobbs was not used to the cold of the northern fall. He tugged at his collar to shield himself from the wind as he walked through the town. Stopping in his tracks quickly, he peered around a corner and was just barely able to see the man in the black coat and derby as he ducked into one of the alleys. Now, he knew for certain that he was being pursued.

He had first noticed it when he left the house where he was staying a few hours ago when he had stopped in at the bakery he enjoyed visiting regularly. When he left with the hot, crusty rolls wrapped in paper, he saw the same man leaning against a wall. When Cobbs turned, the man began heading in a different direction.

He was very close now; Cobbs was being followed. He only needed a few more days and his way would be clear. He had but to collect the treasure from its hiding place where he was staying, make his way to Canada, and then he would be out of danger, and quite a bit wealthier as well. The thought of losing it all now was enough to make one go mad.

Cobbs began hurrying along on his route, looking for a place to conceal himself. Ah! There was a nice alley with shadows and trash piled high. Perfect. He ducked down behind some boxes and listened for footsteps. None could be heard.

Just as he began to breathe a sigh of relief, the darkened barrel of a colt pistol was thrust into the side of his head.

"Don't move, Rebel!" the voice exclaimed. "That is, if you value your life," the voice chuckled.

The pursuer lifted his derby, which had been pulled over his eyes, causing Cobbs' jaw to drop. Tobias looked out from beneath the brim with the wickedest of looks in his eyes.

"Well then, Major," he said with a sneer. "We meet again. Imagine that! And now you're a Rebel defector. What shall we do with you? Hmmmm?" he snapped, steam escaping from his nostrils into the frigid air of the December day.

For the first time in a long time, Cobbs was visibly shaken. Actually, he was terrified to the very core of his being. Shaking and sweating despite the cold, he rose to his feet.

"How… How did you… How did you escape?" he stammered, his question tumbling from his lips.

"Well, it certainly was not because of you or your help, that's for certain! I used an old act I saw a possum perform once. I played dead and was thrown into a pit with the rest of the bodies. I'm not sure that I wouldn't have been better off dead, but I kept still as they threw dirt on us. After I waited a fair amount of time, I poked my head above the thin layer they covered us with. Seeing that I was outside of the camp with no one in sight, I made for the woods. Some kindly slaves took me in until I was nursed back to health, and then I made it my business to hunt you down! I swore the moment you had me taken away that I would get my revenge, and I will have it! Right here, and right now!" And with that, he raised his gun, pointing the lengthy barrel at the spot between Cobbs' eyes.

"Wait! Wait! I'll show you the treasure! I'll split it with you!"

The gun was lowered slightly.

"Oh sure you will, Cobbs! How can I trust you after you left me to rot in that hell hole of a prison camp!"

"I swear; I'll show you! I'll split it evenly! Please, you must believe me!" he pleaded.

Tobias considered for a moment. "How can I trust you? What assurance do I have?"

"Well... I'll give you some of the treasure now! I swear, just pocket your gun and I'll give you the lion's share of what I've got hidden!"

"You'll tell me first! Then, I'll see about letting you go!"

Seeing no other choice, Cobbs was only moments away from revealing his hiding spot when a ruckus broke out on the street. A horse whinnied as it reared up on its hind legs, attempting to avoid crushing an older lady who had wandered into its path. The wagon driver did all he could to control his nag as the general commotion brought people running from the stores that lined the larger street.

In the instant that Tobias' attention was turned away, Cobbs fled further down the alley and reached the fence which closed off the alcove from the next street. He had just clambered to the top when Tobias turned his attention back to his former captor and pointed his pistol while shouting, "Cobbs!"

Cobbs slowly climbed down and faced his tormentor.

"Tobias," he began with a smile. "Old friend. We've been through so much! We'll be rich together! We'll work together to..."

He never had the chance to finish his sentence. With a wicked grin, Tobias pulled the trigger. The shot split the chill air and reverberated through the dark alley. Smoke billowed from the gun's barrel as Cobbs' body hit the ground, already cold.

His lifeless eyes stared into the abyss as Tobias lifted his collar, thrust the gun into his coat pocket, and pulled his hat back over his eyes. He gave one last look at the Major's still form before straightening his coat and walking off into the bright morning air, feeling lighter than he had in years.

Chapter 16

Hans disembarked from the train and looked around at his old home town. It wasn't really a town however, as it was more like a burgeoning industrial hub. The streets were teeming with folks, and the factories were humming with steady business. He felt a jolt of nostalgia as he passed the corner where he had stood on so many cold days, hawking papers. He was glad to be home at last, after four years and some odd months in hell. There was a lingering sense of sadness though. Not so much regarding what had happened to him and what he had seen during the war, but rather the end of the action. He was, after all, someone who craved adventure and danger, and scorned boredom and monotony.

As Hans turned the corner towards home, his ears were still ringing with the incessant chatter of a young boy on the train who had refused to stop blathering about cameras and how one day every person would own one. His mother looked on with embarrassed pride as her son droned on and on. He learned that the boy's name was George Eastman at some point on the trip from Albany. It was sheer dreaming, as any of the cameras he had seen from Brady's photographers were far too complicated and hulking to be owned by just anyone.

As he neared his house, his throat became constricted, and a tear fell from his eye. He was about to see his parents again, and the steps leading to his boyhood home creaked familiarly as he ran up them. The butterflies in his stomach became aggressive as he reached for the door knob.

Hans wasn't sure what he'd find. He hadn't heard from them for some time. The last time had been in the form of a short letter from his mother saying that his father was getting sicker. He had almost cried as he read it in the muddy trenches of Petersburg, but that was nearly a year ago. He had wanted to write back, but the war had gotten in the way of life, much like it had a tendency to do very often.

Now, as he pushed the door open, a smell he was unaccustomed to, filled his nostrils with curiosity. It reminded him of a sort of Russian cooking that he had tasted once or twice during his long service in the army. He found it very odd to smell such a thing in his own home. His parents were German, and this smelled nothing like the Bavarian style of food that his mother usually prepared.

As he entered the kitchen, a sharp-looking Russian immigrant raised his eyes towards him, like he was an unwelcome visitor.

Hans was the first to speak, despite his shock. "Wh... What are you doing here? Who are you?"

"Name's Friedman. Moses Friedman," the immigrant said with a thick Russian accent. "And what might your name be, young man?"

"Hans," he gulped. "Hans Heller. What are you doing in my house?" he blurted.

"Your house? This is my house! I bought it fair and square, and I have the deed to prove it!"

"My family lived... Wait... What has become of my family?"

"Oh! That is, how you say, funny. Your family lived here? A very righteous man named Mr. Heller is who I purchased it from. Made sure we paid no interest too; classy fellow. If you're in search of them though, you can find them on Richard Street in the biggest house!"

After nearly fainting, Hans ran out of the house while making some unintelligible remarks aimed at the still-smiling Friedman. He ran along Boardman Street and turned right at the end. Swinging around wildly, he looked about for the largest house. One home towered above the others, so he ran towards it at full speed, and as he got closer and ran faster, his vision became a blur of trees and dirt.

Hans bounded up the double wide steps, not pausing to announce himself, and burst into the foyer of the massive house.

His father, hale and hearty as he'd ever seen him, rose from the books he'd been studying.

"My son has returned! Mother! Hans is home!"

Mrs. Heller nearly ran through the swinging kitchen doors to embrace her son.

Hans ran towards his parents, and lifting them up in his arms, embraced both of them in a crushing hug. Tears flowed and exclamations resounded through the great hall that was the entrance to the home.

When the family had composed themselves, they all sat around the dining room table, smiling. Hans looked around in amazement and asked to no one in particular, "Where did all of this come from? How did you become so... so wealthy?"

Mr. Heller began with the modest voice that he had always been known for. "Well, Hashem is to thank for all of this. You see, when the war was going on, I realized that we needed to come up with an efficient way of making a living. I couldn't work, and your mother needed to stay home to take care of your younger brothers and sisters.

The only resource we had was our house on Boardman Street, and since there were so many transient and displaced persons roaming around, I thought we could rent out a room or two.

For the first year or so, things went along sluggishly. It wasn't easy, but your mother and I were able to look after the boarders' wants by working hard. Then, a tall man with a mustache and a funny way of talking showed up and asked to rent a room.

He didn't ask twice about the price and even paid a week ahead. We were happy to have him, but he rarely showed up to the meals we regularly served for our guests. He preferred to stay in his room or go out to the bakery down the block now and again.

After about two weeks however, he disappeared completely. We waited several days before asking the police to look for him, but they couldn't discover anything.

We decided to pack up his things so we could rent out his room again. As we put everything in your old wooden chest, we noticed that a floorboard under the bed was out of place, and a small piece of yellow cloth was sticking out from it. After moving the bed, we discovered that a few boards had been moved and then replaced over a hole in the floor. It looked as if it were freshly created.

I reached in, and with some trouble, pulled out a heavy burlap sack, the chord that closed it had been that yellow piece of fabric I noticed. Its weight shifted unevenly as I pulled it over to the dining room. I dumped its contents out over the table, and to our surprise, a huge mound of gold coins and gems fell from it!

Incredible as it sounds, it is true! We quickly placed everything back in the sack and I ran to the Rabbi to ask him about the status of something that was left in our house by a boarder.

Rabbi Bernberg suggested we wait a few weeks for the owner to come back and if he did not, he told us that we would be able to keep what we found according to Halacha. He also recommended that we ask the local authorities about it just to be sure. 'Dina de' Malchusa Dina'[30] as you know.

So, I contacted the law, and they said that since it was in our house, if nobody came to claim it, we had no reason to not keep it.

I put everything in a safe at the bank and we waited.

Two weeks later, when no one had come to ask about it, the treasure became ours! We bought this house, sold our old one, and our monetary troubles seem over."

Hans, whose mouth opened wider and wider during the story, couldn't resist slapping his leg and exclaiming, "Tatty! Trust in God! He will come through!"

His father just sat back in his chair and smiled.

THE END

---

[30] The law of the land is the law even if Jewish law may be lenient in certain cases.

Wooden engraving of the Confederate General John Hunt Morgan

John Pope as a brigadier general

"I have come to you from the West, where we have always seen the backs of our enemies, from an army whose business it has been to seek the adversary and to beat him to when he was found; whose policy has been to attack and not defense.... Let us look before us, and not behind. Success and glory are in the advance; disaster and shame lurk in the rear."
From his order to the "Officers and Soldiers of the Army of Virginia", July 14

General James Longstreet

Captain Henry Wirz

The execution of Henry Wirz, commandant of the (Confederate) Andersonville Prison, near the US Capitol moments after the trap door was sprung.

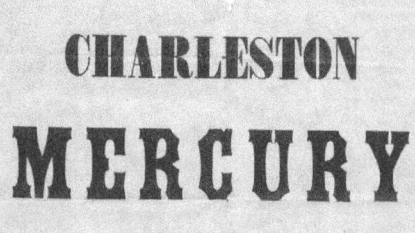

CHARLESTON
MERCURY

EXTRA:

Passed unanimously at 1.15 o'clock, P. M. December 20th, 1860.

AN ORDINANCE

To dissolve the Union between the State of South Carolina and other States united with her under the compact entitled " The Constitution of the United States of America."

We, the People of the State of South Carolina, in Convention assembled, do declare and ordain, and it is hereby declared and ordained,

That the Ordinance adopted by us in Convention, on the twenty-third day of May, in the year of our Lord one thousand seven hundred and eighty-eight, whereby the Constitution of the United States of America was ratified, and also, all Acts and parts of Acts of the General Assembly of this State, ratifying amendments of the said Constitution, are hereby repealed; and that the union now subsisting between South Carolina and other States, under the name of " The United States of America," is hereby dissolved.

THE
UNION
IS
DISSOLVED!

Original copy of the first Confederate imprint announcing that South Carolina formally seceded from the United States of America. 20th of December 1860

Currier & Ives--Second battle of Bull Run.

Prisoners and their "Housing" at Andersonville. Notice the "Death Line" railing. Touching it meant getting shot by one of the guards

A sketch of Andersonville Prison by John L. Ransom

"Shenandoah Valley," oil on canvas, by the artist William Louis Sonntag. Courtesy of the Virginia Historical Society.

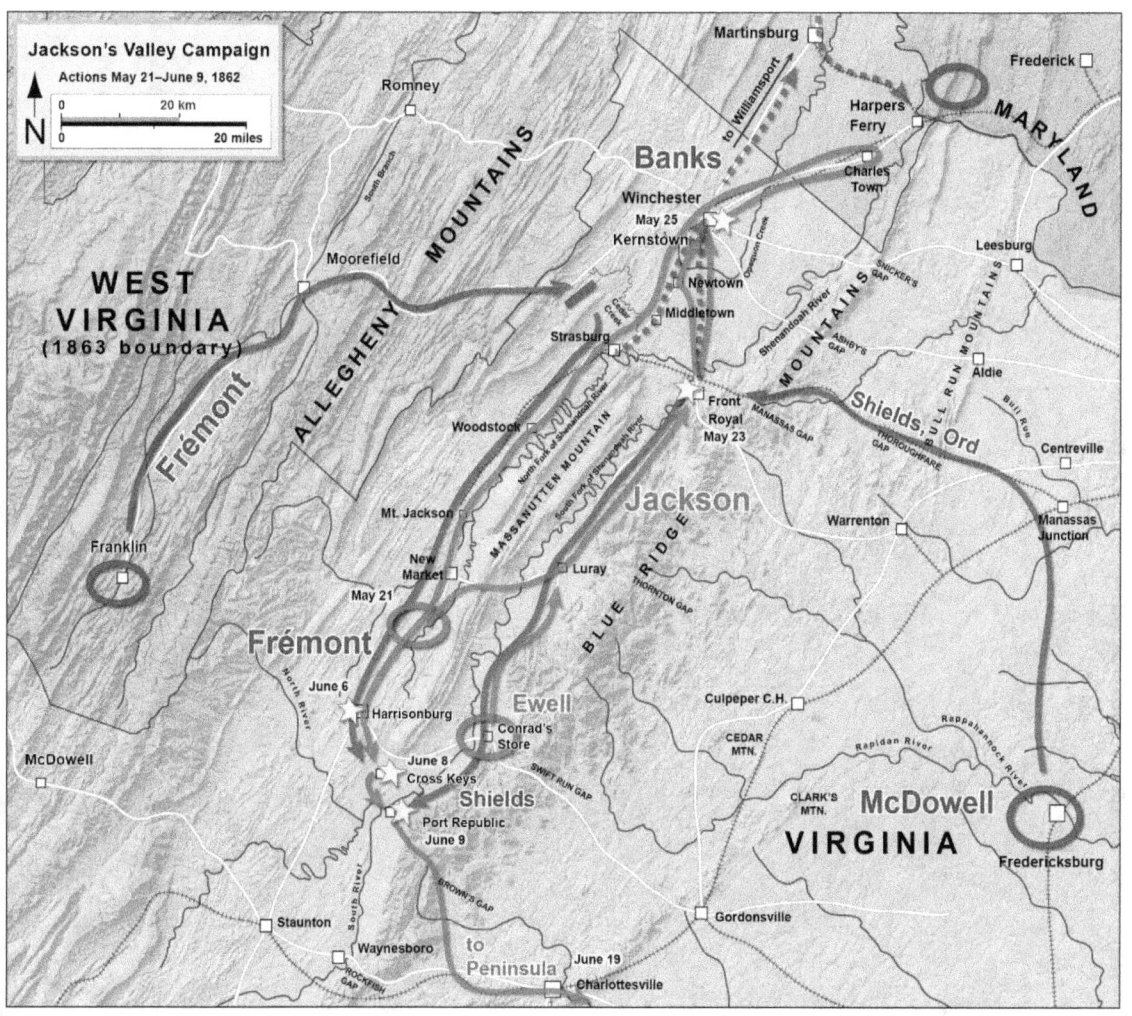

Jackson's Valley Campaign
Actions May 21–June 9, 1862

N

0   20 km
0   20 miles

Martinsburg

Frederick

to Williamsport

Romney

Harpers Ferry

MARYLAND

Banks

Charles Town

WEST VIRGINIA
(1863 boundary)

Moorefield

Winchester
May 25
Kernstown

Leesburg

Newtown

Middletown

ALLEGHENY MOUNTAINS

Strasburg

Shenandoah River

BLUE RIDGE MOUNTAINS

SNICKER'S GAP

ASHBY'S GAP

Aldie

Fremont

Woodstock

MASSANUTTEN MOUNTAIN

North Fork of Shenandoah River

South Fork of Shenandoah River

Front Royal
May 23

MANASSAS GAP

Shields, Ord

THOROUGHFARE GAP

Bull Run

Centreville

Jackson

Mt. Jackson

Warrenton

Manassas Junction

Franklin

New Market

Luray

THORNTON GAP

May 21

Fremont

BLUE RIDGE

June 6

Harrisonburg

Ewell

Conrad's Store

Culpeper C.H.

CEDAR MTN.

Rapidan River

Rappahannock River

McDowell

North River

June 8
Cross Keys

SWIFT RUN GAP

Shields

Port Republic
June 9

CLARK'S MTN.

McDowell

VIRGINIA

Fredericksburg

South River

Staunton

BROWN'S GAP

Gordonsville

Waynesboro

ROCKFISH GAP

to Peninsula

June 19

Charlottesville

133

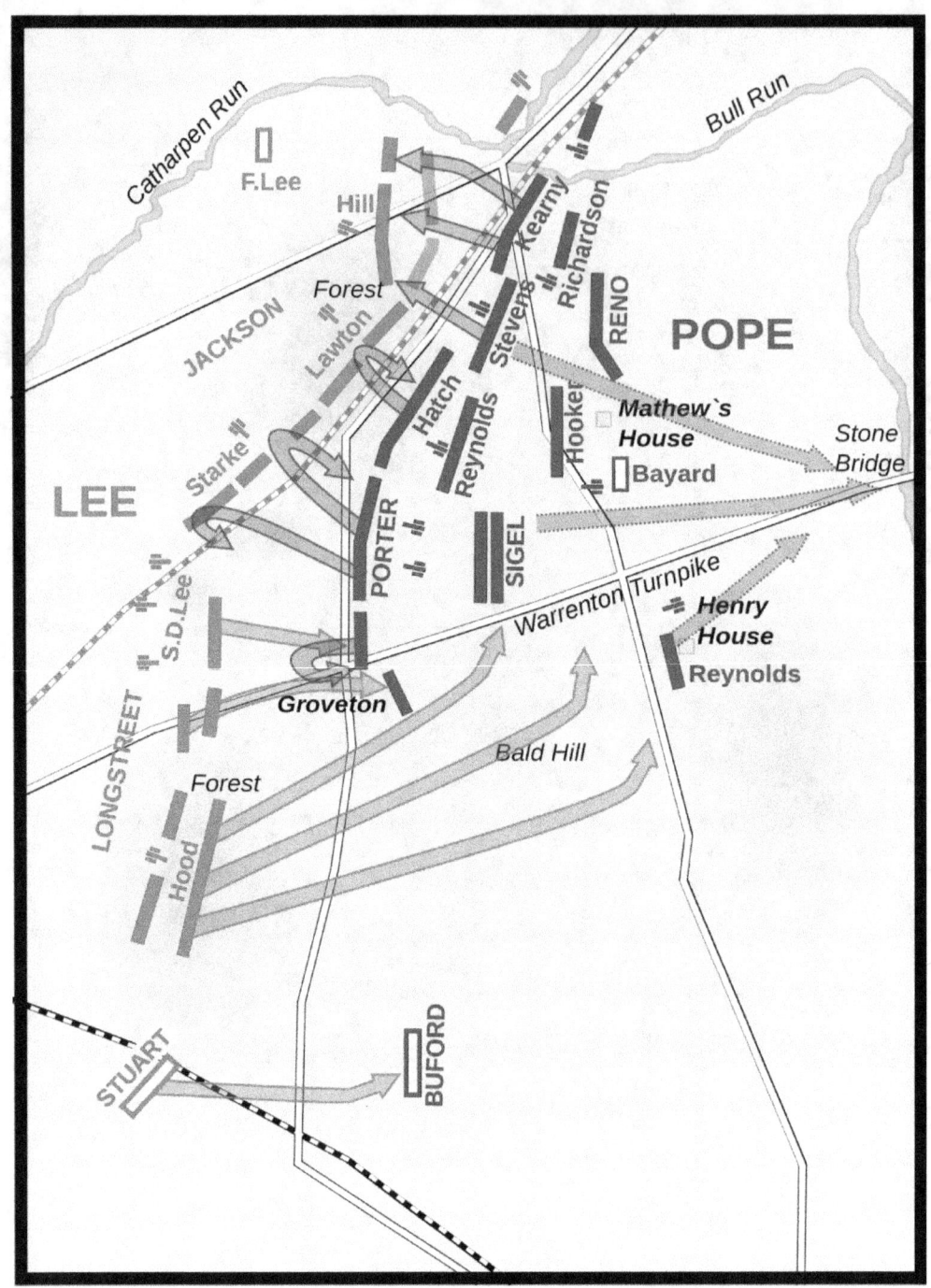

Battle Map of the 2nd Battle of Manassas; where Lee defeated Pope

Historical Note

Of all of the old and dusty tomes that grace the packed (and rickety) bookshelves of my Brooklyn residence, my favorites, and those that I continue to turn to when my interest in other subjects wanes, are those focused on the American Civil war and those about Jewish history. The point at which these two subjects meet has, in my very humble opinion, shaped the current history of our nation and the Jewish people all over the world. I know that I am not in alone in this belief. I've often thought about why that is.

The idea that a nation born in freedom, and according to its own constitution, is dedicated to the preservation of that freedom from tyranny, could possibly have allowed slavery to flourish seems an anachronism, belonging to an earlier feudal type government. In this massive transformation, which caused the demise of over half a million soldiers and countless other civilian casualties that have never been recorded, a new nation was forged. The Civil War eradicated the "curious institution" of slavery, and at the same time changed the United States from a collection of states sharing a common heritage into a nation with a strong, central federal government; changed from the United States "are" to "The United States is".

This new nation was more open to outsiders, which led to the mass immigrations from Western Europe and later Eastern Europe, both of which have shaped our own present in innumerable ways. The Jewish people were instrumental in bringing about this change, holding very important posts in government on both sides of the conflict. Judah P. Benjamin as secretary of war serves as an excellent example of Jewish political involvement.

Several thousand Jews served in some military capacity, achieving ranks as high as Major General on the Union side. I believe that without the Jewish ethos, the fairness inherent in the Jewish law that has been passed down for 3500 years, slavery never would have been eradicated.

The Jewish view on slavery as espoused in the Talmud, a voluminous work on Jewish law, which has been in existence for 1500 years, states very clearly, "One who acquires a slave, acquires a master." The Bible itself has very strict rules as to the treatment of slaves as human beings and not mere chattel. These very concepts were the basis of the abolitionist movement. It may not have always come as direct involvement, but the Jewish Bible is the basis for most of the world's major religions and has worked its way into the legal documents of most nations in one form or the other.

The conclusion that I've come to is probably unique to myself, but through discussion and thought, I think a serious reader and fan of history may be able to shape their own thoughts and conclusions. That was one of the major purposes of my work on this collection of stories.

It is my sincerest hope that our understanding of history's past occurrences will help all of us create a brighter future for all mankind.

Bibliography

Below are some of the more important books and websites, listed in no particular order, which contributed to the stories contained herewith. A careful reader will notice some similarities between some of the character's words and those found in the first hand accounts in Battle and Leaders, specifically the account of Jackson's Chancellorsville campaign entitled Stonewall's Last Campaign by Rev. James Power Smith (Volume III, page 203 Battles and Leaders). You may want to peruse these books if you wish to gain a greater understanding of both subjects. Happy reading!

Civil War Books:

1. McPherson, James M. (2003) [1988]. *Battle Cry of Freedom: The Civil War Era*. Oxford University Press. ISBN 978-0-19-503863-7.
2. Series: Battles and Leaders of the Civil War Publisher: Castle Books; New edition edition (April 1, 1990)ISBN-10: 0890095698
3. T. Harris Williams, Lincoln and His Generals; 1952; 1st edition (1952) Publisher: New York: Alfred A. Knopf, 1952 ASIN: B005KDQ8SU;
4. Foote, Shelby, Reprint edition (1986) *The Civil War A Narrative ;* Vintage; ISBN-10: 0394749138
5. Greer, Walter, Copyright 1926, CAMPAIGNS OF THE CIVIL WAR; Out of print but available from private sellers, for example here: http://www.trocadero.com/stores/mimisantiques/items/1233654/item1233654.html
6. Elisha Hunt Rhodes (author) Robert Hunt Rhodes (editor) ; (July 28, 1992); All for the Union: The Civil War Diary & Letters of Elisha Hunt Rhodes; Publisher: Vintage; 1st Vintage Civil War Library ed edition; ISBN-10: 0679738282

Websites:

1. http://www.jewish-history.com/civilwar/ This is a great site to glean some basic knowledge about the role of Jews during the Civil War. It is well set up as it divides the biographical sketches and material by North and South, Union/Confederate. If you read closely, you may be able to find the inspirations for two of the main characters in the stories.

2. http://www.civilwar.si.edu/ There is no better place to find authentic Civil War information than the https://www.wikipedia.org/Institue and their collection is second to none.

3. https://www.wikipedia.org/ Invaluable when it came to writing this book. The amount of information, maps and photos is incredible. There are those that discount Wikipedia as nearly worthless because anyone can update it. Firstly, because everyone is able to update the site I believe it actually adds to the accuracy. If someone questions the information, it is flagged and unless there is a reliable reference it will be called into question. It is like a collective effort that allows for more accuracy, not less. Secondly, what was used up until the advent of the internet were books, which are typically one person's opinions; perhaps the editors and that's it. Therefore, the writer's agenda may have been pushed over the actual truth. Just my opinion of course but I believe there is some merit to it.

Images:

The images contained within this work are considered public domain in the United States. This applies to U.S. works where the copyright has expired, often because its first publication occurred prior to January 1, 1923.

Abraham's Shield

- "ChancellorHouseChancellorsville1863" by Unknown - File from The Photographic History of The Civil War in Ten Volumes: Volume Two, Two Years of Grim War. The Review of Reviews Co., New York. 1911. p. 126.
- "Darius N. Couch." Library of Congress description: "Gen. D.N. Couch, U.S.A." - Matthew Brady
- "Dowdall's Tavern - Howards Headquarters during the battle until driven from it by Jackson's assault on May 2, 1863." File from *The Photographic History of The Civil War in Ten Volumes: Volume Two, Two Years of Grim War*. The Review of Reviews Co., New York. 1911. p. 125.
- "General J. E. B. Stuart." J. Gurney & Son - This image is available from the United States Library of Congress's Prints and Photographs division under the digital ID ppmsca.38003
- "Lithograph of the death of General Jackson." Publisher - Kurz and Allison in Chicago, IL.
- "General Daniel E. Sickles." This image is available from the United States Library of Congress's Prints and Photographs division under the digital ID cwpb.05563

- "General Joseph Hooker." Library of Congress Prints and Photographs Division. Brady-Handy Photograph Collection. http://hdl.loc.gov/loc.pnp/cwpbh.00839. CALL NUMBER: LC-BH82- 1397
- "Gen. O. O. Howard (between 1855 and 1865)." Library of Congress, Prints and Photographs Division, Brady-Handy Collection, reproduction number LC-DIG-cwpbh-00893.
- "General Robert E. Lee." Julian Vannerson - The Library of Congress Prints & Photographs Online Catalog; http://www.loc.gov/rr/print/catalog.html

Jonah Revisited

- "Chromolithograph depicting the Battle of Hampton Roads." Morgan Riley.
- "Ruins of Tredegar Ironworks, Richmond, Va. April, 1865." Brady National Photographic Art Gallery (Washington, D.C.) (1858 - ?), Photographer (NARA record: 1135962)
- "The CSS Hunley." Sketch by R.G. Skerrett. 1902

A Letter Home

- "General George G. Meade." Photoshop cleanup of Library of Congress (1860s public domain) photograph by Mathew Brady. TITLE: Gen. George G. Meade CALL NUMBER: LC-BH82- 4428 <P&P>[P&P] REPRODUCTION NUMBER: LC-DIG-cwpbh-01198
- "General John F. Reynolds." Unknown Photographer.
- "Hancock at Gettysburg" L. Prang & Co. print of the painting by Thure de Thulstrup, showing Pickett's Charge. Restoration by Adam Cuerden. The copyright holder of this file, Adam Cuerden, allows anyone to use it for any purpose, provided that the copyright holder is properly attributed. Redistribution, derivative work, commercial use, and all other use is permitted.

The Bouquet

- "A Currier and Ives depiction of a battle during the Siege of Petersburg." This image is available from the United States Library of Congress's Prints and Photographs division under the digital ID cph.3b53122
- "Confederate entrenchments during the siege of Petersburg." This image is available from the United States Library of Congress's Prints and Photographs division under the digital ID cwpb.02790
- "Ruins in Richmond." Albumen print. Photographer Russell, Andrew J.

Where it all Belongs

- "Wooden Engraving of the Confederate General John Hunt Morgan." This image was published in: (1864-09-24). "The Late General John Morgan," Harper's Weekly VIII
- "John Pope as a Brigadier General." Photographer unknown. Published prior to January 1, 1923
- "General James Longstreet." Photographer unknown. Published prior to January 1, 1923
- "Captain Henry Wirz." Photographer unknown. Published prior to January 1, 1923
- "The execution of Henry Wirz." This image is available from the United States Library of Congress's Prints and Photographs division under the digital ID cwpb.04196 The author died in 1882, so this work is in the public domain.
- "Original copy of the first Confederate imprint announcing that South Carolina formally seceded from the United States of America." 20th of December 1860
- "Prisoners and their 'Housing' at Andersonville." Photographer unknown. Published before 1923 and public domain in the US.
- "A sketch of Andersonville Prison." by John L. Ransom. This image is available from the United States Library of Congress's Prints and Photographs division under the digital ID pga.02585
- "The second battle of Bull Run, fought Aug. 29th 1862." Published by Currier & Ives, [1862?] New York
- "Shenandoah Valley," oil on canvas, by the artist William Louis Sonntag. Courtesy of the Virginia Historical Society.

All Maps

- Maps by Hal Jespersen, www.cwmaps.com

About the Author

William Evans spends his days as the marketing manager for a Brooklyn Car Company and then steps into a phone booth during the evening (remember those?) and emerges as a writer. Okay; so maybe that's not exactly true, but what is true is the fact that he is passionate about writing, storytelling, and history—and hopes that his books will teach, as well as entertain. He holds a bachelor's degree in Talmudic law and is an avid runner, artist, and music-head. He lives in Brooklyn with his lovely wife and five kids.